UNIT A

LIFE CYCLES

Theme: Models

D1455819

A1

GET READY TO

OBSERVE & QUESTION

How do adult animals care for their young?

Animals are all around you. Close observation will help you learn about them. How do the animals you observe care for their young?

EXPERIMENT & HYPOTHESIZE

How do plants change during their life cycles?

Measuring the trunk of a tree can help you find out the age of the tree. What else can you discover about how plants grow?

INVESTIGATE!

RESEARCH & ANALYZE

As you investigate, find out more from these books.

- **INSECT METAMORPHOSIS *From Egg to Adult*** by Ron and Nancy Goor (Atheneum, 1990). Do you know how to recognize a moth at any stage in its life cycle? This book will tell you how.

- **Tree in a Forest** by Jan Thornhill (Simon and Schuster Books for Young Readers, 1991). If a maple tree could talk, it would probably tell the story in this book. Read the book to find out about that story.

WORK TOGETHER & SHARE IDEAS

How can you give your pets and plants the best care possible?

Working together, you'll have a chance to apply what you have learned about plants and animals. Share the information your group finds out. Look for the opportunities in Unit Project Links to include your ideas in an Animal Sitter's Guide and a Plant Sitter's Guide.

CHAPTER 1

LIFE CYCLES OF ANIMALS

Think about some animals that you know. What were they like when they were young? How did they change as they grew older? Do you think all members of the animal kingdom grow and change throughout their lives?

Flying With a Bear

Would you like to be alone in a small plane with a large bear? Jay Hammond, a bush pilot and biologist, was flying high above the Alaskan wilderness. Suddenly his passenger, a 275-kg (600-lb) bear, started to awaken. The bear had been drugged to keep it calm during the flight.

As the pilot dropped out of the clouds and searched for a place to land, the bear grew restless. Minutes later, Hammond unloaded the bear on the shore of a lonely lake. Now wide awake, the animal ran off to find a new home. Here the bear will mate, raise cubs, and spend the rest of its life. Like all animals, it will grow and change. How are animals alike in the ways they change? How are they different? To find out, read this chapter!

Coming Up

◄ Bush pilot Jay Hammond flew a bear to its new home.

WHAT IS A LIFE CYCLE?

Arrange these words in order—*teenager, child, adult, baby*. How did you do it? Each word names a stage in the life cycle of a human. All living things go through stages, or life cycles. In this investigation, you'll find out about the life cycles of some plants and animals.

Activity

The Changes Chart

How have you changed since you were a baby? How do other living things change during their life cycles? Find out.

MATERIALS
- strip of white paper
- pictures of plants and animals
- books about animals
- *Science Notebook*

Procedure

1. With your group, brainstorm a list of living things that you've observed near your home or school. **Record** your list in your *Science Notebook*.

2. Make a Changes Chart. Fold a strip of paper lengthwise into four sections. First, fold the strip in half. Then fold the folded strip in half.

3. Choose a living thing from the list you made in step 1. In the first section, at the left of the chart, **draw** a picture or **write** a description of how you think the plant or animal looked when it was very young. For help, look at pictures in books. **Predict** how the plant or animal will change as it gets older.

4. In each of the other three sections of the chart, **draw** or **write** your ideas about how the animal will change. Do not name the animal.

5. Exchange Changes Charts with another group. Study the other group's chart. Name the plant or animal that this chart is about. Ask the other group if you guessed correctly.

Analyze and Conclude

1. **Make a plan** to test your predictions from steps 3 and 4.

2. Show your teacher your plan. Then carry it out. How do the predictions you recorded on your Changes Chart **compare** with what you found out?

INVESTIGATE FURTHER!

EXPERIMENT

Fold a paper strip into eight sections. In the sections write these ages: 1, 3, 5, 7, 9, 15, 25, 55. Write how you have changed in the sections. For the ages you have not reached, predict how you will change. Explain your predictions.

Step 3

City Life

A city is full of life. People, spiders, ants, birds, dandelions, squirrels, roses, and earthworms are only a few of the things that live in a city. You might have to look closely to see some forms of city life. But if you observe the living things in a city over time, you'll notice that they change.

Think of the Changes Chart you made in the activity on pages A6 and A7. All living things—whether they live in a city, a town, an ocean, a forest, a desert, or your home—go through certain changes. These changes include growth, development, reproduction, and death. Growth refers to changes in size— that is, plants and animals becoming larger. Development refers to changes in plants and animals as they mature, or become adults. Reproduction is the process by which plants and animals produce offspring, or young, of their kind. Death marks the end of each plant's or animal's lifetime.

Animals go through ordered life stages, as you can see in the pictures of the dogs below. After several

PUPPIES Puppies are born and then grow.

Life Cycle of a Dog

ADULT Puppies develop into mature, or adult, dogs that reproduce, or have puppies.

▲ **Living things in the spring**

years, an adult dog dies. But because it has reproduced, that kind of dog continues.

Plants go through life stages, too. A milkweed plant grows, blooms, and produces seeds. Some seeds fall to the ground. From these seeds new plants grow. The mature plant dies. But because it has reproduced, that kind of plant continues.

Look at the two pictures above and below. What living things can you find? Compare the pictures. What changes have taken place in the living things over time?

The ordered stages that occur in a plant's or animal's lifetime are called a **life cycle**. A life cycle is like a circle. It has no end. One life cycle leads to another. ■

Living things in the summer ▼

What's Wrong
With This Picture?

If you heard that a duck had hatched out of a chicken egg, you probably wouldn't believe it. It's a fact that animals produce young just like themselves. Chickens mate and produce chicks. Ducks mate and produce ducklings.

Chicks belong to one species (spē'shēz) and ducks belong to another species. A **species** is a group of living things that can pro- duce living things of the same kind. Now do you know what's wrong with this picture?

Passed On or Learned?

Animals of the same species pass on certain traits. A trait is a charac- teristic. It describes something. You and your classmates belong to the human species. You all have many of the same traits.

Some things are not passed from parents to offspring. These things are learned. For example, having feet is a human trait that is passed from parents to children. But using your feet to kick a soccer ball is a skill you learn. Chicks hatch knowing how to peck for food. But suppose a chick pecks at a caterpillar that tastes bitter. Then the chick learns to avoid that kind of food.

How Long Do Animals Live?

By producing young, each species can continue beyond the life span of each parent. An animal's life span is the time between its birth or hatching and its death.

Species	Life Span
Spider	1-20 years
Gray Squirrel	8-15 years
Cat	12-15 years
Eagle	20-30 years
Elephant	65 years

As you can see in the table above, each species' life span is different from another's. A spider's life span is only one to twenty years. Yet box turtles have been known to live as long as 123 years. ■

INVESTIGATION 1

1. Think about how a life cycle and a circle are alike. What must happen so that the life cycle of a species does not end?

2. Choose an animal and draw a picture of two different stages in its life. Order the stages by labeling them 1 and 2.

WHAT IS THE FIRST STAGE IN AN ANIMAL'S LIFE CYCLE?

A newborn kitten and a newborn puppy look *so* tiny. But each developed from something much tinier. What is that something? Find out and become an "eggs-pert" as you explore the first stage in an animal's life cycle.

Activity

Be "Eggs-act"!

To a scientist, observing something means much more than just looking. In this activity you must be "eggs-act" as you explore the first stage in a chicken's life cycle.

Procedure

1. Think of an uncooked egg cracked into a dish. **Make a drawing** in your *Science Notebook* to show the inside parts of the egg that you remember. If you can, label each part. Mark the drawing *A*.

2. Get an uncooked egg from your teacher. With your group, use a hand lens to **observe** the outside of the egg. **Draw** what you see.

3. Crack the egg into a dish. Use the hand lens to **observe** the egg and the inside of the shell. **Draw** all the parts that you see. Mark this drawing *B*.

4. **Compare** drawing *A* with drawing *B*. What new parts did you discover?

Analyze and Conclude

Step 3

1. Based on the drawings your class did, do you think that all chicken eggs have the same parts? A chicken is a kind of bird. Do you think that all bird eggs have the same parts? How could you find out?

2. Each part you observed has a different job. Find the white spot on the yellow part of the egg. This spot could have developed into a new chick. **Infer** how the eggshell helps the developing chick.

INVESTIGATE FURTHER!
....

EXPERIMENT

Observe the eggs of another animal—for example, a fish. How are these eggs different from chicken eggs? How are they the same?

Step 3

A13

"Eggs-traordinary" Eggs!

Do you think eggs "eggs-ist" only to boil, poach, scramble, or fry? Actually, the job of an egg is to help produce offspring, or young. An **egg** is the first stage in the life cycle of almost all animals. Some animals—for example, baby horses—develop from eggs inside their mothers' bodies. Other animals—for example, chickens—develop from eggs outside their mothers' bodies.

Eggs are "eggs-traordinary" in many ways. Even the tiniest egg contains everything needed for developing a new animal. Study the parts of the egg shown. Add labels to drawing *B*, which you made in the activity on pages A12 and A13.

"Eggs-actly" How Would You Describe an Egg?

Eggs come in many shapes, colors, textures, and sizes. Chicken eggs are round on one end and pointed on the other. Owl eggs are round. Plover eggs are pear-shaped. Tortoise eggs are shaped like globes and sand grouse eggs like tubes.

These photos show the actual sizes of some of the many kinds of bird eggs. ▼

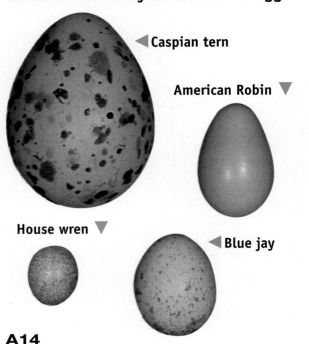

◀ **Caspian tern**

American Robin ▼

House wren ▼

◀ **Blue jay**

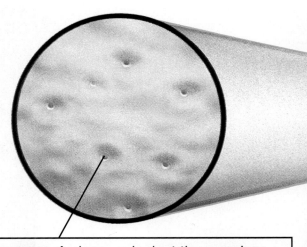

PORES A close-up look at tiny openings, called pores, in the shell of a chicken egg. Pores let water and oxygen enter the egg and carbon dioxide leave.

Eggs can be brightly colored, dull, plain, or very fancy. From green and blue to black and red, eggs can be freckled, speckled, spotted, or dotted.

There are many kinds of egg coverings, too. Bird eggs have hard, chalky shells. Fish and frog eggs have a soft outer covering. They don't dry out, because they're laid in water. Slug and snail eggs have shiny, round shells that you can almost see through.

Inside a Bird Egg

TWISTED STRANDS Twisted strands of the shell lining keep the embryo upright as the mother turns her egg. Turning the eggs warms them evenly.

SHELL The egg is covered by a shell. The shell protects everything inside the egg. A material called calcium makes the shell hard and helps to form the embryo's bones.

EMBRYO The white spot is where the embryo begins to grow as soon as the egg is laid. The **embryo** is the developing chick. By the twenty-first day, the chick will start to hatch.

EGG WHITE The egg white cushions the embryo and provides it with water.

YOLK The yolk is the stored food for the embryo.

SHELL LININGS Just inside the shell are the shell linings. At the rounded end of the egg is an air space, which allows the embryo to get oxygen.

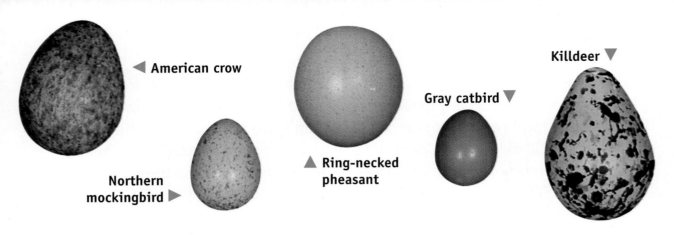

◄ **American crow**

Killdeer ▼

Gray catbird ▼

▲ **Ring-necked pheasant**

Northern mockingbird ►

Ostrich eggs are the largest in the world. Each ostrich egg is 16 cm (6 in.) long and has a mass of about $1\frac{1}{2}$ kg (3 lb). Compare this with the hummingbird egg in the picture below.

"Eggs-actly" How Many?

The number of eggs that an animal lays varies with the species.

INVESTIGATE FURTHER!

EXPERIMENT

You can't easily see pores in a shell, but you can prove they are there. Place an egg in a clear container. A brown egg is best to use. Cover the egg with water. Observe the egg after 20 minutes. You may need to use a hand lens. Everywhere you see a bubble on the shell, there's a pore. Each bubble is formed by carbon dioxide gas that's passing through a pore from inside the shell.

The hornbill lays only 1 egg a year, but an oyster lays 500 million eggs a year. Chickens lay almost 1 egg a day, or up to 350 eggs a year. Each time an ocean sunfish produces eggs, it makes about 300 million.

Not every egg produces young. The eggs you eat do not contain embryos. For a chick or other animal to begin growing inside an egg, the mother must first mate with the father. Then—just think—the egg can grow into all the parts of an animal's body. An egg really is "eggs-traordinary"! ■

A tiny hummingbird egg compared with an ostrich egg ►

Hatching Chicks

An incubator (in'kyŌŌ-bāt ər) is a device that provides enough warmth, water, and fresh air to help keep something alive. An incubator in a hospital may help a tiny baby grow stronger. Other incubators are found on large chicken farms. These incubators are used to hatch eggs. Incubators for eggs, like the one shown here, come in two parts—the setter and the hatcher. Read the captions to find out the difference. ■

The trays in the setter move to turn the eggs many times each day. Eggs are warmed to a temperature of 37°C (99°F).

Large fans keep the air moving around the eggs.

1 SETTER Chicken eggs are placed on trays and loaded into a setter. Some setters are as large as rooms and can hold thousands of eggs at one time. The eggs stay in the setter for 18 days.

2 HATCHER On the nineteenth day, the eggs are put into metal or plastic baskets and moved to the hatcher. After 2 or 3 days in the hatcher, baby chicks hatch out of the eggs.

The Baby Book

Almost all animals come from eggs. Some animal babies develop from eggs inside their mothers' bodies. Those babies are born live. Other offspring develop from eggs outside their mothers' bodies. Those babies hatch. Whether born live or hatched, each baby develops from a single egg.

Here are some baby animals from around the world. Look at the pictures and read about them. Which were born live? Which hatched?

Baby African elephants grow inside their mothers' bodies for nearly two years. When a baby elephant, called a calf, is finally born, it weighs as much as a fully grown man. ▼

WALLABY

▲ Wallabies, from Australia, are members of the kangaroo family. A baby wallaby is called a joey. It is born live. Then it wriggles into its mother's pouch, where it drinks its mother's milk. The joey stays there until it is about eight months old.

This mother crocodile from Egypt carries her hatched babies into the water to protect them from enemies. She will crack the eggs that are slow to hatch inside her mouth and let the babies wiggle into the water. ▼

ELEPHANT

CROCODILE

BEAR

OWL

◀ This bear cub had a mass of less than $\frac{1}{2}$ kg (1 lb) when it was born. The rings of fur around its eyes make it look as if it's wearing spectacles, or eyeglasses. The spectacled bear is the only kind of bear that lives in South America.

These baby snowy owls hatched in a nest on the ground. Their home in the far north is a cold place called the tundra (tun'drə). Both parents care for their chicks. All the chicks are born with white fluff, which later turns gray. The gray color blends in with the ground and helps to hide the young owls from enemies. ▶

PENGUIN

◀ Gentoo penguins live in the Antarctic. They make their nests out of rocks. The penguin parents take turns sitting on the nest. Both parents feed and care for the chicks that hatch. When the young penguins are about eight to ten weeks old, they swim out to sea and live on their own.

— INVESTIGATION 2 —

THINK IT WRITE IT

1. On page A15 you read about the parts of an egg. Think about each part and what it does. For each part, explain what would happen to the egg if that part didn't work.

2. The first life-cycle stage is the same for animals that hatch and animals that are born live. Describe that stage.

HOW DO SOME ANIMALS GROW AND CHANGE?

Have you ever worn a costume and found that no one knew you? As some animals go through their life cycles, they change so much that you may not know what animals they are. Find out about two ways animals grow and change.

Activity

Look at What You've Become

Imagine how you will change as you grow up. Do all animals change in the same ways you do? The animals in this activity are masters at some amazing changes. Find out what they are.

MATERIALS

- goggles
- plastic gloves
- 5 mealworms
- dry cereal without a sugar coating
- thin slices of apple and potato
- dish with a cover
- hand lens
- metric ruler
- *Science Notebook*

SAFETY

Wear goggles and gloves when handling the mealworms. Wash your hands when you have finished.

Procedure

1. Look at the list of materials with your group. **Predict** what a mealworm needs in order to survive. Explain which material meets which need. **Infer** which material might provide a mealworm with water.

2. Use the materials to make a home for the mealworms. In your *Science Notebook*, **describe** the home you made. Place the mealworms in the home.

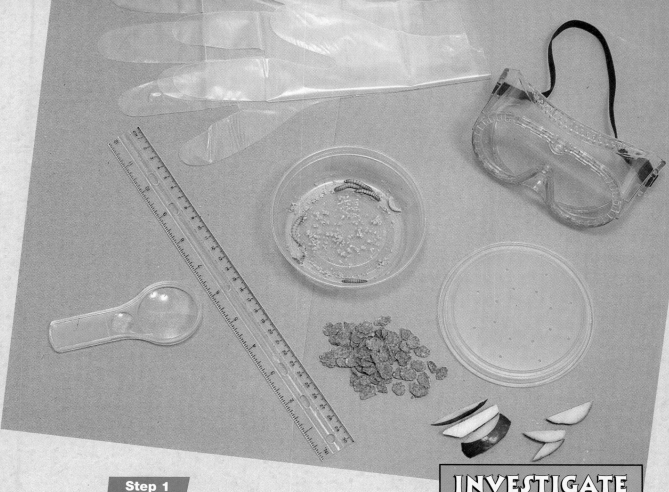

Step 1

3. Every two days, clean the home and give the mealworms fresh food.

4. **Observe** the mealworms with a hand lens each day for three weeks. Use a ruler to **measure** changes in size. **Record** any changes you observe.

Analyze and Conclude

1. How did the mealworms change?

2. The adult stage of this insect is called a beetle. How many different stages did you observe in the life cycle of the mealworm beetle? **Draw** each stage.

INVESTIGATE FURTHER!

EXPERIMENT

Pet store owners keep mealworms in a refrigerator. Find out how a cold temperature affects a mealworm's life cycle. Use two mealworms. Keep one cold and the other at room temperature. What did you observe? What conclusions can you draw about the effects of cold temperatures on a mealworm's life cycle?

Activity

That's Something to Chirp About!

Crickets are insects that are found in dark, damp places, such as under logs and rocks, in bushes, in deep grass, and in other shaded areas. Make a home for crickets and observe them as they grow and change.

MATERIALS

- goggles
- plastic gloves
- 2 terrariums, each with a lid that has holes in it
- apple slices, lettuce, small pieces of cracker
- damp sand
- small plastic dish
- hand lens
- crickets
- *Science Notebook*

SAFETY

Wear goggles and gloves when handling the crickets. Wash your hands when you have finished.

Procedure

1. You're going to make a home for crickets from some of the materials provided. Look at the list of materials. With your group, **predict** what a cricket needs in order to survive. Explain which material meets which need. **Hypothesize** which material might provide water.

2. Make a home for the crickets. Be sure to put a small plastic dish, to serve as an egg chamber, in the home. When you have finished, place the crickets in their home.

3. Every two days, clean the home and give the crickets fresh food.

4. Every day, **observe** the egg chamber carefully for eggs. In your *Science Notebook*, **record** the day you first find eggs.

Step 2

5. Use another box and other materials to make another cricket home. Move the egg chamber into the new home. Provide food near the eggs.

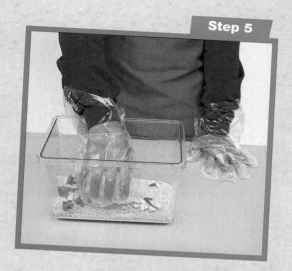

Step 5

6. Watch for the eggs to hatch. Some kinds of crickets take much longer to hatch than others. **Record** the day the eggs hatch. The young crickets are called **nymphs** (nimfs). When the nymphs can hop, place them with the adult crickets.

7. Use a hand lens to **observe** the crickets. **Compare** the adult crickets and the nymphs. **Record** what you observe.

Step 7

Analyze and Conclude

1. How are the nymphs like the adults? How are they different?

2. What different stages did you **observe** in the cricket life cycle?

3. How does a cricket's life cycle differ from a mealworm's?

INVESTIGATE FURTHER!

EXPERIMENT

Observe the nymphs as they grow. What happens to them? Record what you find out.

Going Around in Cycles

▲ From one birthday to the next, people grow and change. How has this person changed?

Your life cycle is very simple. You are first a baby, then a child, then a teenager, and then an adult. Suppose you saw a baby picture of an adult friend. You'd probably be able to say who the baby in the picture grew up to be. But if you saw an insect such as a butterfly in an early stage, you might not know what the animal was.

A Four-Stage Cycle

There are four stages in the life cycles of most species of insects. The stages in order are (1) egg, (2) larva, (3) pupa, and (4) adult.

Life Cycle of a Butterfly

LARVA A larva, called a caterpillar, hatches from the egg. It sheds its outer covering several times as it eats and grows.

PUPA The caterpillar makes a covering called a chrysalis (kris′ə lis). This is the pupa stage.

ADULT After developing fully, an adult butterfly comes out of the chrysalis.

EGG The female adult mates, lays eggs, and the cycle starts over again.

A four-stage life cycle is called **complete metamorphosis** (met ə-môr′fə sis). The first stage is the egg. The second stage, called the **larva** (lär′və), is a wormlike stage that doesn't look at all like the adult. The larval stage of certain insects has a special name. Look at the pictures on this page. What is the butterfly larva called?

The larva eats and grows and then makes a covering for itself. At that time, the insect is in the third stage, called the **pupa** (pyo͞o′pə). Inside the pupa, the adult insect develops. When it is fully developed, the adult insect comes out. The **adult** is the last stage of a life cycle. The adult female insect then mates and lays eggs, starting the cycle again.

The beetle also goes through complete metamorphosis in its life cycle. In the activity on pages A20 and A21, you observed mealworms, the larvas of beetles. The larva of the mealworm beetle is called a grub.

Now you can see that an insect in some stages doesn't look at all like the adult. A caterpillar certainly doesn't look like a butterfly. And a mealworm doesn't look like a beetle.

A Three-Stage Cycle

There are three stages in the life cycles of some insects. The names of the stages in order are (1) egg, (2) nymph, and (3) adult. A three-stage life cycle is called **incomplete metamorphosis**.

As with all animals, the first stage in the life cycle is the egg. The animal in the second stage, called a **nymph**, looks almost like a small adult. As the nymph eats and grows larger, it sheds its outer covering several times and then develops into an adult.

Then the female adult lays eggs that can go through the same cycle. Look at the pictures of the life cycle of a grasshopper. In what ways is the nymph like the adult grasshopper? How is it different?

A cricket goes through incomplete metamorphosis. On pages A22 and A23, you did an activity with crickets. How are cricket nymphs and grasshopper nymphs alike?

Science in Literature

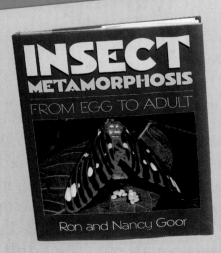

INSECT METAMORPHOSIS FROM EGG TO ADULT
by Ron and Nancy Goor
Atheneum, 1990

Did you know that after a caterpillar sheds its skin, it has to puff up the new skin with air, like a balloon? That's one of the strange but true facts about the life cycles of insects told in *Insect Metamorphosis: From Egg to Adult*.

As you read this book and examine the close-up photographs, think about what amazes you the most. Make a list of strange but true metamorphosis facts. Share your list with your family and friends. Were they also amazed?

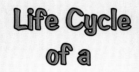

Life Cycle of a Grasshopper

NYMPH A nymph hatches from an egg. The nymph looks almost like the adult, but it is smaller and has no wings. As the nymph eats and grows, it sheds its outer covering several times.

ADULT Finally, after 40 to 60 days, the nymph has developed into an adult. Most adult grasshoppers have wings. The adult female mates and lays eggs, and the cycle continues.

EGG The female adult lays eggs in a hole that she digs in the ground.

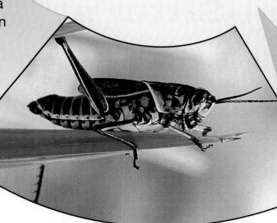

INVESTIGATION 3

THINK IT WRITE IT

1. When a frog hatches from an egg, it has a tail that it later loses. Then it looks like an adult. Tell whether the frog's life cycle is complete or incomplete metamorphosis and explain why.

2. Compare the life cycles of two animals—one that goes through complete metamorphosis and one that goes through incomplete metamorphosis.

HOW DO ADULT ANIMALS CARE FOR THEIR YOUNG?

Have you ever had a sitter? Hiring a sitter is one way adult humans might care for their children. In this investigation you'll learn how animals differ in the ways they care for their young.

Activity

The Animal-Sitter's Guide

What's a sitter's job? Suppose an animal such as a baby whale or a young giraffe had a human sitter. What do you think that sitter would need to know to care for the young animals? In this activity you'll find out.

Procedure

1. Take a card from your group's animal-sitting assignment box. Look at the name of the animal on the card and **record** the name in your *Science Notebook*. Find out about the baby animal's needs and how the parents care for the baby. **Record** what you find out. **Infer** the care the baby animal should receive.

panther

hawk

turtle

Step 1

2. On a sheet of construction paper, write a list of instructions for an Animal-Sitter's Guide for the class. Give information that would answer questions such as these: What kind of food does the baby animal need? When does it sleep? Does it make unusual noises? What might threaten or harm the baby animal?

3. Include a drawing or picture of your animal.

4. Put your instructions in the class Animal-Sitter's Guide, where others can refer to them.

Analyze and Conclude

1. What would be the hardest part of taking care of the animal you wrote about? Explain your answer.

2. **Compare** the care needed by your animal with the care needed by other baby animals in the Guide. Which animal would be the hardest to sit for? Which would be the easiest? Explain your answers.

Step 2

UNIT PROJECT LINK

Pet owners are like full-time animal sitters. Predict which pets are hardest to care for. With your group, interview owners of different kinds of pets. Find out about the pets' care. Record the information in a special pet section of your Animal-Sitter's Guide.

Out of Sight, Out of Mind

It's easy to forget about something that you can't see. "Out of sight, out of mind" is a short way to say this. You might use this saying to describe how some animals behave toward their eggs. For example, a cowbird lays her eggs, one at a time, in the nests of other, smaller birds. Then she flies away. The "foster parent" birds hatch, feed, and care for the young cowbirds. You can see that for the mother cowbird, her eggs are "out of sight, out of mind."

Many Eggs—Few Survive

Frogs and most fish lay many eggs but don't protect them. A frog lays thousands of jelly-covered eggs. Many frog eggs become food for other animals, such as the cat-eyed snake of North and South America. The frog eggs that survive develop into tadpoles. Some of the tadpoles also become food for snakes. But others survive.

Some animals hide their eggs before leaving them. A female sea

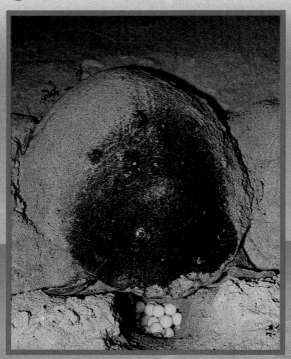
2 The female lays her eggs.

1 A female sea turtle swims to shore.

turtle crawls out of the sea at night. Using her flippers as shovels, she digs a nest, in which she lays at least a hundred eggs. Then she covers the eggs with damp sand. When daylight comes, she crawls back into the sea and never sees her young.

Although she has laid many eggs, probably only one baby turtle out of a hundred will survive. Other animals, such as raccoons, steal eggs from turtle nests. When the eggs that survive do hatch, the baby turtles crawl toward the sea. But sea birds swoop down upon them for food. And many of those that reach the water become food for sea animals.

Survival Kit

How do animals that hatch from out-of-sight, out-of-mind eggs sur-

▲ **A Colorado potato beetle and its eggs on a potato plant**

vive? One thing that helps cowbirds survive is that the adult females lay their eggs in nests of smaller birds. Because the young cowbirds are larger than the other young birds in the nests, they get more food.

Other animals lay their eggs at food sources. A Colorado potato beetle lays its eggs on a potato plant. The larva hatches just when the potato leaves are ready to eat. ■

3 The baby turtles hatch.

4 The baby turtles crawl to the sea.

A Whale of a Baby

Did you know that the world's biggest baby is about 8 m (26 ft) long and has a mass of about 1,800 kg (2 T)? It's longer than a station wagon and weighs as much as a small truck. This baby is a blue whale calf. The blue whale calf's mother is much bigger than her baby. She's about 30 m (100 ft) long and has a mass of over 90,000 kg (100 T). That's as long as two big tractor-trailers and heavier than the largest dinosaur. A land animal's legs couldn't support that mass. But ocean water can.

A Whale of a Birth

A whale develops inside a mother whale and then is born live. Whales are born underwater in early winter, almost a year after the mother and father mate. A mother whale is called a cow. The baby is a calf. Normally, the calf slithers out of the cow's body tail first.

The mother watches the newborn calf float to the surface. There the calf takes its first deep breath and sends up a fountain of mist from the blowhole on top of its head.

A mother humpback whale with her calf ▼

From the time it is born, the calf can swim. For several weeks the calf swims close to its mother. She gently strokes the calf with her flipper. A mother whale never leaves her baby unattended. She watches as it takes in fresh air before diving and as it blows out its warm breath when surfacing.

To feed, the calf dives underwater, where its mother squirts rich, warm milk into its mouth. A blue whale calf drinks about 500 L (132 gal) of milk every day and gains about 90 kg (200 lb) a day.

A Whale of a Journey

One kind of whale is called a humpback. During the winter, the mother whales never eat. They live off their stored fat. But in the spring, thousands of whales head for the colder waters of the Arctic, where there is food. The whales swim in small groups called pods. On this long journey north, the mother whale watches out for dangers. Killer whales can hurt and even kill a baby whale. A whale can get caught in nets dragged by fishing boats. Then it can't swim to the surface to breathe. A mother whale will protect her baby even if it means putting herself in danger.

▲ **A closeup look at baleen**

A Whale of a Summer

By summer humpback whales arrive at the Arctic. The waters there are their feeding grounds. Since the mother whale hasn't eaten for six months, she's hungry. She will eat a year's worth of food—probably a ton a day—in the next six months.

Humpback whales don't have teeth. Instead, they have baleen, or flat bony plates that hang down from the roof of the mouth like the teeth of a comb.

Humpback whales feeding
(*top and right*)

The mother whale gulps big mouthfuls of sea water. She closes her mouth part way and then squirts the water out. She swallows the food that is trapped by the baleen. A whale's mouth can hold a ton of food.

All summer, as the mother whale eats and her calf drinks milk, they build up layers of fat. They play together. They slap the water with their tails. They roll over. Sometimes the little whale breaches—it hurls itself out of the water, twists high in the air, and lands with a splash!

A Whale of a Whale

In the fall the whales travel south toward warmer waters. There the calf's mother may mate again.

The young humpback whale has grown strong. It can find its own food. Now only a year old, it has doubled its birth size. It is truly a whale of a whale. ■

INVESTIGATION 4

1. Think of a particular kind of very young animal. Suppose you found such an animal, and it was separated from its parents. Write how you might help care for the baby animal.

2. Choose an animal you have learned about in this investigation. Describe the care that the animal gets as it grows and develops.

REFLECT & EVALUATE

WORD POWER

adult   life cycle
egg   nymph
embryo   pupa
larva   species
complete metamorphosis
incomplete metamorphosis

On Your Own
Review the terms in the list. Then use as many terms as you can in a paragraph about life cycles.

With a Partner
Make a list of all the terms that apply to people. Have your partner list all the terms that apply to a butterfly. Compare your lists.

BUILD YOUR PORTFOLIO

Find out about an animal's life cycle. Glue pictures or make drawings on a large sheet of paper to show the animal's life cycle. Draw arrows to order the stages. Write the name of the animal below the life-cycle pictures.

Analyze Information

Study the photograph. Then use the photograph to name and describe all the stages in this insect's life cycle. Does the insect go through complete metamorphosis or incomplete metamorphosis? Explain.

Assess Performance

Make up a new kind of animal. Draw the egg of the animal, what the animal looks like when it is young, how the animal changes as it grows, and what its parents look like. Name your animal and label each picture.

Problem Solving

1. A mother sea turtle may have a hundred babies at one time. But a mother elephant gives birth to only one baby at a time. How do you think a mother elephant and a mother turtle might differ in the ways they care for their babies?

2. How might your life be different today if you had skipped the development that occurs between the ages of two and four in your life cycle? Tell why all the stages of growth in a person's life are important.

2

LIFE CYCLES OF PLANTS

Many members of the plant kingdom grow from seeds. Have you ever planted a seed and watched it grow into a plant? What happened to the plant as time passed?

A Child, a Plant, a Poem

Gwendolyn Brooks, an African American poet, tells in this poem about a child who plants a seed.

Tommy

I put a seed into the ground
And said, "I'll watch it grow."
I watered it and cared for it
As well as I could know.
One day I walked in my back yard
And oh, what did I see!
My seed had popped itself right out
Without consulting me.

—Gwendolyn Brooks

In this chapter you'll learn how plants grow and change. And you'll discover other things plants do "without consulting you."

Coming Up

◀ **Planting flowers**

WHAT IS THE FIRST STAGE IN THE LIFE CYCLE OF A FLOWERING PLANT?

What a survival story! In Egypt, seeds buried for over 1,000 years were able to start a new life cycle. You'll dig up more about seeds in Investigation 1.

Activity

The Inside Story

Seeds come in many sizes. But even the smallest seed can begin a new plant life cycle. Find out what's inside a seed.

- -

Procedure

1. Use a toothpick to pry open the halves of one lima bean seed. With your group, **observe** the parts of the seed. Place the two halves so that their inside surfaces are facing up. **Draw** the two halves in your *Science Notebook*. **Draw** arrows that point to each part. Number the arrows.

MATERIALS

- goggles
- soaked lima bean seeds
- toothpicks
- water
- paper towels
- 2 sealable plastic bags
- stapler
- metric ruler
- tape
- hand lens
- *Science Notebook*

SAFETY

Wear goggles during this activity. Clean up any spills immediately.

Step 1

2. Place a piece of wet paper towel in a plastic bag. Staple the bag about 2 cm from the bottom. Pry open a second bean seed and separate the two halves. Place all four seed halves in the bag.

3. Prepare a second plastic bag like the first one. Add four whole bean seeds to the bag. Seal both bags and tape them to a wall or bulletin board. **Record** the date.

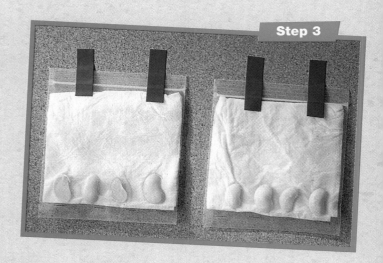

Step 3

4. Use a hand lens to **observe** the whole seeds and seed halves each day. **Record** any changes. After three days, remove one of the whole seeds from its bag. Separate the halves. **Record** what you see. Every three days remove another whole seed and separate its halves. **Record** all observations.

Analyze and Conclude

1. What changes occurred in the whole seeds? What changes occurred in the seed halves? **Hypothesize** about what might account for the differences.

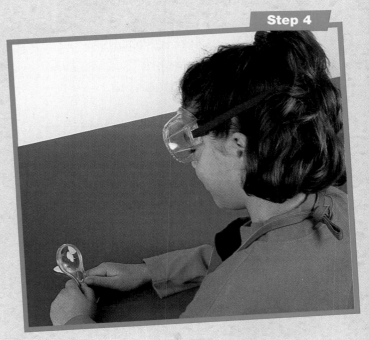

Step 4

2. How many different seed parts did you find? **Describe** each part. Beside each description, write the number that matches the number of the same part on your drawing.

3. Based on your observations, **infer** which seed part provides food for the young plant that grows from the seed. Explain your inference.

Corn
Simply "A-maize-ing"

TIME Capsule

Corn is one of the most important foods in the world. People and many kinds of farm animals eat corn. Corn, also called maize, can be used to make food products, such as cooking oil and bread. The time line shows how important corn has been.

Because the action in World War I has destroyed much of the farmland in Europe, the United States sends ships loaded with food to Europe. Corn and wheat from America save thousands of people from starving.

1920

2000

Farmers grow different kinds of maize and invent better ways to store crops for winter.

800

1995
Farmers grow almost as much corn as they grow wheat.

Maize is planted and harvested in Mexico. This corn is a type of wild plant.

2700 B.C.

1620
The Pilgrims land at what is now Plymouth, Massachusetts. Native Americans show the Pilgrims how to plant, grow, and use corn. The Pilgrims have a day of thanks which we celebrate today as Thanksgiving.

A.D. 200
Maize, along with beans and squash, becomes a main part of people's diets in the Americas. Ways are found to increase the food production.

Plant Tricks

Seeds can do stupendous tricks! Have you ever blown on the fluffy round head of a dandelion? Each little parachute that floats away is a seed that can produce a plant.

The Many Kinds of Seeds

The first stage in the life cycle of a flowering plant is a seed. Seeds are as different as the plants that grow from them. Seeds come in many sizes. A carrot seed is tiny. A coconut is a large seed. Seeds come in many shapes—round, pointed, oval, flat, and thin. They come in many patterns and colors—solid, speckled, white, brown, black, yellow, and red.

Whatever its size, shape, or color, a seed has three parts—a seed coat, stored food, and an embryo (em'-brē ō). Find out about these parts as you study the drawings below.

How Seeds Survive

Seeds are survivors. Plants have grown from lotus seeds that are centuries old. And seeds perform all kinds of tricks. Seeds can burst open, pop out, explode, fly, float, hitchhike, and parachute. These tricks help a seed get away from its parent plant. Then the new plant that develops from the seed will have space to grow.

PARTS OF A SEED

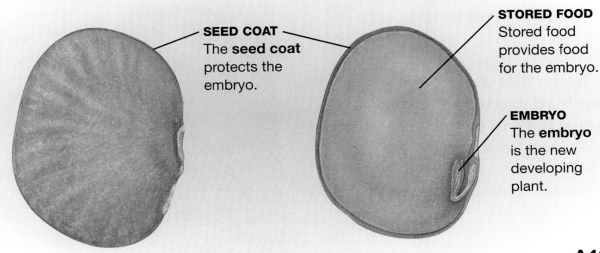

SEED COAT
The **seed coat** protects the embryo.

STORED FOOD
Stored food provides food for the embryo.

EMBRYO
The **embryo** is the new developing plant.

Wind scatters some seeds. As the tumbleweed plant is blown along the ground, its seeds scatter. Wind also blows seeds away from the parent plant. Some seeds have a shape that helps them travel in the wind. Because of its shape, the milkweed seed travels easily in the wind.

Animals also scatter seeds. As animals roam, their fur can pick up and carry seeds. Animals such as mice carry seeds away and bury them. Birds carry seeds on their feathers and in their beaks. People sometimes carry seeds on their clothing.

▲ **Seed in a bird's beak**

What Seeds Need

A seed needs warmth, air, and moisture to **germinate** (jʉr´mə-nāt), or sprout. In the activity you did with seeds, on pages A38 and A39, a wet paper towel in the bags provided moisture for the seeds. When a seed is in the ground, a tiny hole in the seed coat allows moisture to enter the seed. In addition to warmth and water, a seed needs oxygen from the air before it can germinate.

▲ **Milkweed seeds popping out**

Water also scatters seeds. Lotus seeds fall into water and float away. Some settle in the muddy bottoms of rivers and lakes and grow into new plants. Some seeds, such as coconuts, even float across oceans.

▼ **Sticktight seeds in a squirrel's fur**

With the proper conditions, a seedling develops. A **seedling** is a new plant that develops from an embryo. The growing plant has parts that help it get what it needs to grow. Some plants have long tap-roots that can reach far underground for water. Other plants have fuzzy stems and leaves that capture and hold in moisture.

Seed Plants Not From Seeds

All seed plants produce and can grow from seeds. However, some can grow from trailing plant stems called runners or from underground plant parts called tubers (too′bərz). A potato is an example of a tuber. Plants such as tulips can grow from bulbs. Some plants can even grow from a piece of stem or leaf. But all seed plants produce seeds.

Runners, tubers, bulbs, and cuttings don't produce seedlings—only seeds produce seedlings. Seedlings develop into plants that produce food, which is used by the plants and by animals that eat the plants. ■

▲ **A bean seedling**

INVESTIGATION 1

1. In Chapter 1 you found out about the stages in the life cycles of animals. How is the seed stage in the life cycle of flowering plants like the egg stage in an animal's life cycle?

2. Explain how the parts of a seed help a flowering plant produce a new plant.

HOW DO FLOWERING PLANTS MAKE SEEDS?

Have you ever picked or chosen a flower for a friend? What helped you decide which one to take? Was it the scent, the color, or the interesting shapes of its parts? In this investigation you'll find out how each of these is important for flowers to make seeds.

Activity

It's a Flower! It's a Factory!

Have you ever heard about a factory that blooms? A flowering plant is a factory. What does this factory make? In this activity you'll find out about one of its products.

Procedure

1. **Examine** a flower carefully. **Make a drawing** of it in your *Science Notebook*. **Draw** an arrow to each part of the flower. Label any part that you know.

2. Carefully pull the petals apart so that you can see the center of the flower. **Make a drawing** of what you see. Write questions about what you **observe**.

Step 2

3. With your group, **compare** the parts of your flower with the photo shown. Label the parts on both of your drawings.

4. Gently shake your flower over a sheet of plain white paper. The small powdery objects that fall from the flower are grains of **pollen** (päl'ən). Use a hand lens to **observe** the grains. Feel the grains. **Describe** how they look and feel. **Record** your observations.

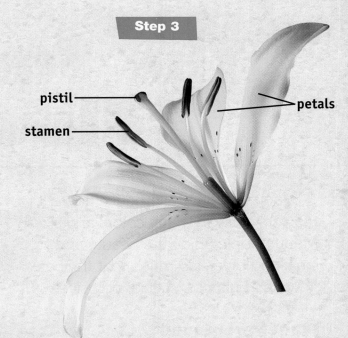

Step 3

pistil

stamen

petals

Analyze and Conclude

1. The **pistil** (pis'til) is the part of the flower where seeds form. Why do you think its location in the center is important?

2. The **stamen** (stā'mən) is the part of the flower that contains pollen. For seeds to form in most plants, pollen must travel from a stamen of one plant to the pistil of another. Use a cotton swab to move pollen from a stamen to the pistil. **Hypothesize** how insects and birds might move pollen. **Talk with your group.** Explain your ideas and **record** your hypothesis.

3. A flower's petals attract insects, which feed on a sweet liquid in the plant. What is it about petals that might attract insects?

Step 4

The Fantastic Flower

Many seed plants produce flowers. Flowers grow in many colors and sizes. Many people enjoy the beauty and smell of flowers so much that they give flowers as gifts on special occasions.

Plant Parenthood

Flowers might be called the parents of plants. A flower is part of an adult flowering plant. Seeds are formed in flowers. It is through the seed that the life cycle of the parent plant can continue.

Each flower has three parts that help a flower carry out its parent role. Their names are pistil, stamen, and petals. Look at the picture as you read about each part.

PARTS OF A FLOWER

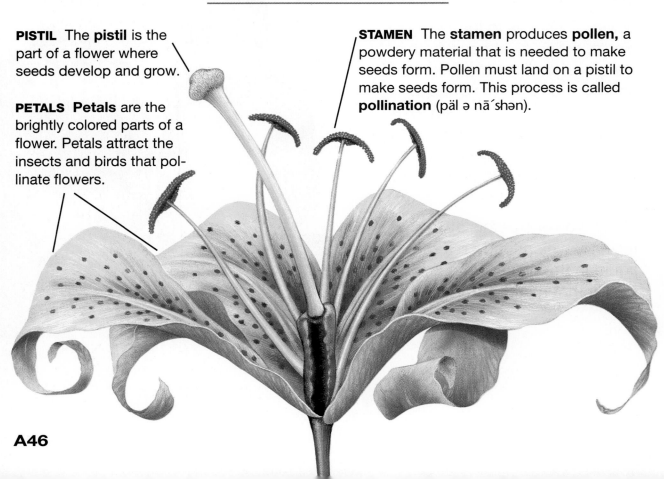

PISTIL The **pistil** is the part of a flower where seeds develop and grow.

PETALS Petals are the brightly colored parts of a flower. Petals attract the insects and birds that pollinate flowers.

STAMEN The **stamen** produces **pollen,** a powdery material that is needed to make seeds form. Pollen must land on a pistil to make seeds form. This process is called **pollination** (päl ə nā′shən).

A46

Seed Protection

Do you like to eat fruit? Did you know fruits come from flowers? A **fruit** is the part of a flower that forms around a seed. Pea pods, tomatoes, and apples are all fruits that we eat. A fruit protects the seed or seeds inside of it.

A fruit also provides a way for the seeds to be scattered. For example, birds like to eat cherries. Inside each cherry is a single seed, which is protected by a hard shell. When a bird swallows a cherry, it digests the soft part of the fruit. But the seed passes unchanged through and out of the bird's body. If the seed falls on the ground, it can grow into a new cherry tree.

Birds also like to eat blackberries, but they do not like blackberry seeds.

▲ **Fruits protect seeds.**

The birds push the seeds aside and wipe them off their beaks. The tiny seeds fall to the ground, where they can grow into new blackberry bushes.

Plant Helpers

Insects help in the pollination of flowering plants. For example, bees are attracted to the bright colors of a flower's petals and to a sweet-tasting nectar (nek′tər) inside the flower.

Each grain of pollen, which you observed in the activity on pages A44 and A45, has a sticky coating. When an insect comes to feed on the nectar in a flower, pollen grains cling to the insect's feet and body. They then carry the pollen to the pistil of the same flower or to the pistil of another flower.

▼ **A tomato is a fruit.**

Not all flowers are pollinated by insects. Sometimes pollen is carried by wind and water. Birds and other animals, attracted by a flower's color and scent, can also carry pollen from one flower to another.

The hummingbird hovers over a flower and pushes its long beak deep into the flower to get the nectar. Pollen from the flower sticks to the bird, which then carries the pollen to the next flower.

Bats help pollinate flowering trees. Bats drink the nectar and eat the pollen. They transfer the pollen stuck on their tongues and noses from flower to flower.

Fantastic Flower Facts

Pollination can occur in some unusual ways. When an insect lands on a redbud flower, its petals spring open. This action allows the insect to reach the pollen and carry it away. Flowers of the American mountain ash, or rowan tree, grow in clusters. Near each cluster, there is a sort of platform where insects can land and then pollinate the flowers. The flowers of the catalpa tree have deep trumpet-shaped tubes. As an insect crawls inside a tube to reach the nectar, the insect picks up pollen.

Plant Cycles

The life cycles of flowering plants vary greatly in length. The life cycles of some trees, for example, may be hundreds or even thousands of years long! Many of the flowering plants you know have yearly life cycles. Such plants are called annuals. Study the life cycle of an annual shown on the next page.

▼ **Flower of a redbud tree**

▼ **Flower of a catalpa tree**

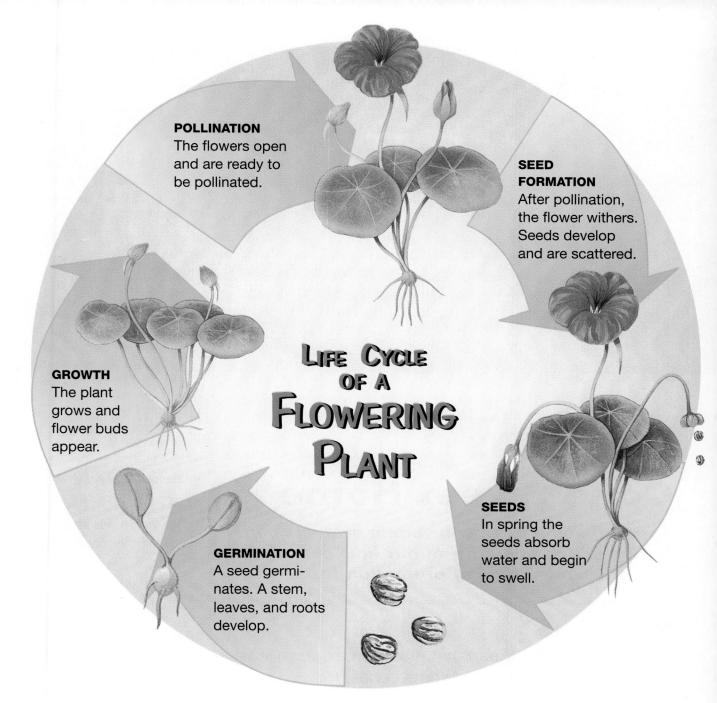

LIFE CYCLE OF A FLOWERING PLANT

POLLINATION
The flowers open and are ready to be pollinated.

SEED FORMATION
After pollination, the flower withers. Seeds develop and are scattered.

GROWTH
The plant grows and flower buds appear.

SEEDS
In spring the seeds absorb water and begin to swell.

GERMINATION
A seed germinates. A stem, leaves, and roots develop.

INVESTIGATION 2

1. Suppose you ordered a bowl of fruit at a restaurant. Your waiter delivers a bowl of sliced cucumbers. Was there a mistake? Explain your response.

2. Describe the three main parts of a flower and tell how each part helps seeds form.

How Do Plants With Cones Make and Protect Seeds?

Have you ever seen pine cones used to decorate something? For a pine tree, cones are more than just decoration. In this investigation you'll find out just what cones do for a plant.

Activity

Cone Sweet Home

Think of some ways your home protects you. In this activity you'll find out how cones provide the same kinds of protection for seeds.

Procedure

1. A cone is a plant part that grows on a tree called a conifer (kän'ə fər). **Examine** some cones. **Record** your observations in your *Science Notebook*.

2. With your partner, **classify** the cones. Each group of cones should share at least one characteristic. Use characteristics such as size, color, and shape.

3. Look at the pictures of conifers on the next page. What kinds of conifers did your cones come from?

Pine cone ▲

Cedar cone ▶

Spruce cone ▶

4. A cone is made of woody parts called **scales**. Carefully pull off several scales from each cone. A conifer seed grows on the scale where the scale joins the cone. With a hand lens, **observe** the scales to find a seed. **Make a drawing** of what you observe on the scales.

Pine tree

Step 4

5. Look at the picture of the cone scale at the right. **Compare** the picture with your drawing.

Spruce tree

Analyze and Conclude

1. Some cones can open and close. They open and release their seeds in dry weather. Cones close in damp weather to protect the seeds from moisture. **Talk with your group** and **infer** what one job of a cone is.

2. How are the cone of a conifer and the fruit of a flowering plant alike?

Cedar tree

A51

Evergreens

Many trees shed their leaves in the fall as part of their life cycles. But other trees have leaves (or needles) all year long. Such trees are called evergreens because they're always green. Actually, evergreens do shed their leaves, but they grow new ones at the same time. That's why they're always green.

Pine, spruce, fir, hemlock, and cedar trees are all evergreens. These trees have something else in common—they all bear cones. A **cone** is the part of an evergreen tree that produces pollen or seeds. Not all evergreens produce cones. But those that do are called conifers. The word *conifer* means "cone-bearing."

There are two kinds of conifer cones. Pollen cones make and release pollen, much as the stamen of a flower does. Seed cones receive

DIFFERENT KINDS OF EVERGREENS

Eastern hemlock ▶

Douglas fir ▶

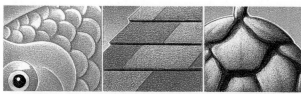

fish scales   roof shingles   cone scales

the pollen and use it to make seeds. Each cone is a woody stalk covered with stiff **scales**, which protect the seeds under them. As you saw in the activity on pages A50 and A51, the scales overlap, like the scales on a fish or the shingles on a roof.

The Life Cycle of a Conifer

What happens to the seeds of cone-bearing evergreens? Some are eaten or carried away by animals.

Others simply fall to the ground. Those seeds that are lucky enough to land on good, rich soil and receive enough warmth, moisture, and sunlight can grow into trees.

One good place for a seed to fall is on a rotting log. The log is rich in things that plants need to grow. So the log nurses the tiny seed as it sprouts and develops into a seedling. A log that feeds a seedling is called a nurse log.

As a seedling's roots grow down and its branches grow out, it develops into a young conifer. The young conifer grows taller and taller and produces cones. At the proper time, the seed cones open and let their seeds go. And the life cycle of the conifer continues.

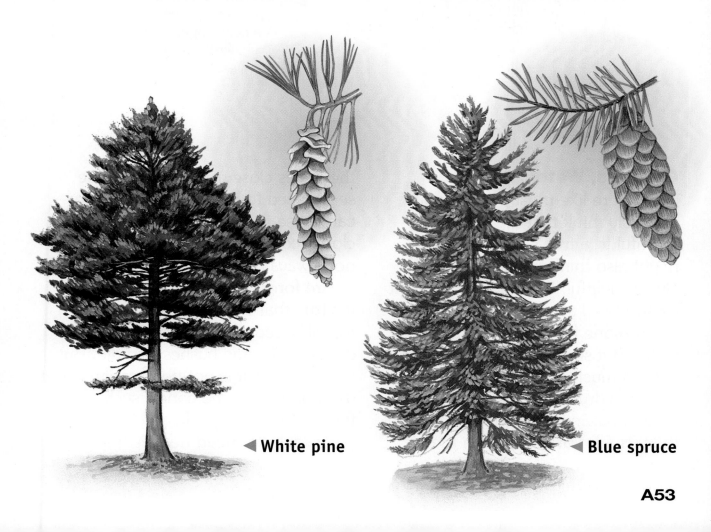

◄ **White pine**

◄ **Blue spruce**

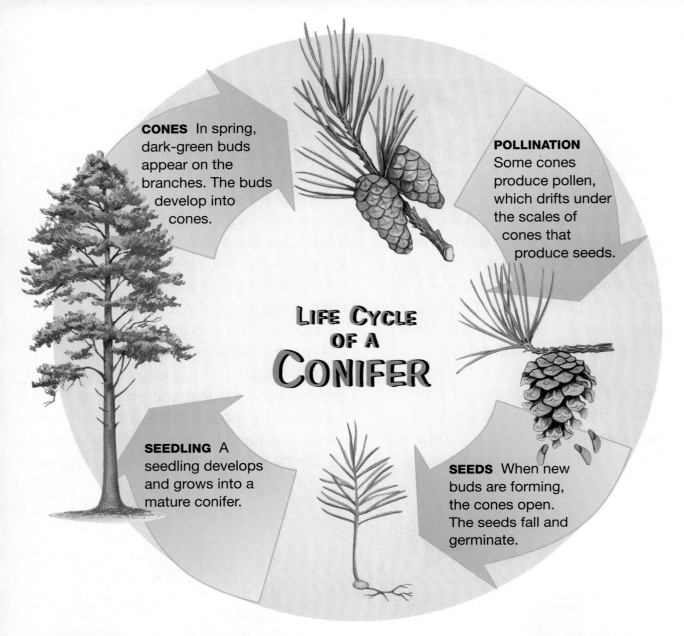

LIFE CYCLE OF A CONIFER

CONES In spring, dark-green buds appear on the branches. The buds develop into cones.

POLLINATION Some cones produce pollen, which drifts under the scales of cones that produce seeds.

SEEDS When new buds are forming, the cones open. The seeds fall and germinate.

SEEDLING A seedling develops and grows into a mature conifer.

Conifers, Water, and Fire

If you're like most people, you probably think that fire is always harmful to a tree's life cycle. You might also think that moisture is always helpful. Read on—you might be surprised at what you find out.

Everyone knows that plants need water. But sometimes, a conifer can get too much of a good thing. When the air is dry, the scales in the cones open, allowing air to enter. When there is a lot of moisture in the air,

the scales close up tightly, because seeds need to be kept dry. Moisture can cause the seeds in a tightly closed cone to rot. So moisture is not always helpful.

Are forest fires always harmful? It's true that when fire hits the leafy top of a tree, the tree almost always dies. Shrubs and bushes also die. But the forest itself is not necessarily dead. In fact, some cones, such as those of the lodgepole and jack pines, actually *need* heat as hot as a

A forest fire ▲   **Soon after the fire** ▲

fire just to open. These cones remain closed until they reach a temperature as high as about 50°C (122°F). The high temperature melts the sticky pitch inside the cone, and the cone opens. Then the seeds can be scattered. Soon some of the seeds germinate, and seedlings appear. Fire may sometimes be harmful to plants but not to cones that contain the seeds for new conifers. ■

Within a year, regrowth begins. ▶

INVESTIGATION 3

1. Think back to what you learned about flowering plants. What part of a conifer do you think is most like the fruit of a flowering plant? Explain your answer.

2. Describe how cones help make and protect seeds. Explain the role a cone can play in the regrowth that takes place following a forest fire.

How Do Plants Change During Their Life Cycles?

You already know some changes that plants make during their life cycles. In this investigation you'll find out how some plants change as they grow and how they respond to changes around them.

Activity

Sizing Up Tree Growth

As you grow, the bones in your legs and arms get longer. What parts of a tree get longer when it grows? Find out.

- - - - - - - - - - - - - - - - - - -

Procedure

1. Look at the tree in the pictures. How did the tree change?

2. **Compare** the two trunks. **Record** your observations in your *Science Notebook*.

3. **Compare** the height of the lowest branch in each picture. **Compare** the length of the branches in each picture. **Record** your observations.

MATERIALS
- metric tape measure
- *Science Notebook*

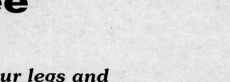

▲ Young tree

▲ Same tree at mature stage

4. The trunk of most trees grows about 2 $\frac{1}{2}$ cm bigger around each year. **Measure** the distance around the trunk of a tree at a height of about 120 cm off the ground. **Record** your measurement. **Estimate** the age of the tree.

5. Find out how branches grow. The place on a branch where growth is occurring usually has a different color from the rest of the branch. **Observe** some branches on two different kinds of trees. Look for color differences. Where do they occur? Remember to look at the branches, not the leaves. **Record** what you observe.

Step 4

Analyze and Conclude

1. Based on your observations, **infer** where growth occurs on a branch. What happens to the branches of a tree as the tree ages?

2. How do the trunks of most trees change as the trees age?

INVESTIGATE FURTHER!

RESEARCH

How can you tell when a tree is sick or dying? Call a tree service and find out, or research diseases of trees in an encyclopedia or book about plants. What changes caused by disease would you look for? What might cause the death of a tree? Share your findings with your class.

Activity

A Change of Plants

Do you squint when you walk into bright light? Find out how plants respond to changes in their environment.

- -

Procedure

1. Put one seedling into a shoebox. Put the lid on the box. Be sure the seedling is away from the hole in the lid.

MATERIALS

- goggles
- 3 seedlings, each growing in a paper cup
- shoebox with a lid that has a hole in it
- plastic wrap
- tape
- *Science Notebook*

SAFETY //////

Wear your goggles. Wash your hands after handling seedlings.

Step 1

2. Use a pencil to make a small hole in a sheet of plastic wrap. The stem of a seedling should just fit through the hole. Gently pull the seedling in the second cup through the hole. Tape the plastic wrap tightly to the cup, as shown.

3. Gently turn the cup upside down. Tape the cup to the bottom of a shelf or a desk-top so that the seedling hangs upside down, as shown.

4. Place the third seedling on a flat sur-face where it can receive light.

5. **Talk with your group** and **predict** how each seedling will look in three days. **Record** your predictions in your *Science Notebook*.

6. After three days **observe** the seed-lings. **Record** any changes you observe.

Analyze and Conclude

1. **Compare** your observations with your predictions. What do you think caused any changes you observed?

2. If a plant could not adjust to changes, **infer** what might happen to it.

Step 2

Step 3

UNIT PROJECT LINK

Sometime you might be asked to plant-sit for a friend's plants. Ask people you know if they have had any problems in caring for their plants. Find out how the problems were solved. Record the problems and solutions in a Plant-Sitter's Guide.

Where Are You Growing?

As you get older, you get bigger. As a plant goes through its life cycle, it gets bigger, too. The stem gets taller. The roots get longer. The roots and shoots grow more branches. All plants, from a tiny violet to a giant redwood tree, grow in these ways.

Plants, like the trees you observed in the activity on pages A56 and A57, also grow in another way. Their stems get bigger around. Imagine hugging a tree. You can reach around the trunk of a young tree. But you may not be able to do this after the tree has been growing for many years.

Responding to Light

If a bright light is shined in your eyes, you'll squint. Plants respond to light, too. Have you ever seen a photograph of a field of sunflowers? You may have noticed that all the flowers are turned the same way.

Plants respond to light by growing toward it. Recall how the seedlings grew in the activity on page A58. If a plant is placed where it gets light on only one side, the stem of the plant

will bend in the direction the light is coming from.

Responding to Water

In many places enough rain falls to supply plants with the water they need. But in the desert, water is very scarce.

The cactus, a desert plant, has long roots near the surface of the soil. They collect water from a wide area. The cactus also has a thick stem that stores water and keeps it from evaporating.

Amaryllis growing toward light ▶

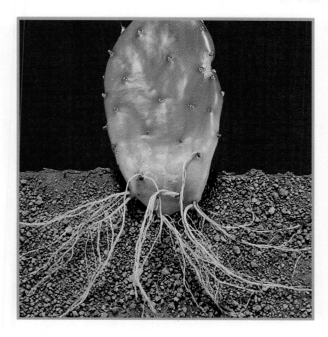

▲ **Cactus roots growing toward water.**

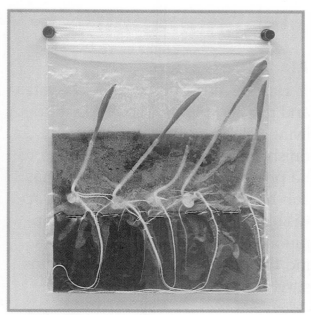

▲ **Roots grow down and stems grow up.**

Responding to a Pull

Roots and stems respond to the force called gravity, which pulls you toward Earth. Roots grow in the direction of the pull of gravity. So they grow down. Stems grow in the direction opposite to the pull of gravity. So they grow up.

SCIENCE IN LITERATURE

A TREE IN A FOREST
by Jan Thornhill
Simon and Schuster, 1991

Jan Thornhill tells the amazing story of the life of a maple tree in words and colorful paintings. Find out how a tree grew and changed over its 212-year lifetime.

After reading the book, retell the story in a life cycle diagram. Look back at the one on page A54 in this book to see an example. In your diagram, show what the tree looked like at important stages of its life. Use the years written at the bottom of some pages in *A Tree in a Forest* to help you label your diagram.

Plant Protection

Besides responding to light, water, and gravity, plants also respond to living things in their environment. To finish their life cycles, plants need to be protected from living things that can harm them. Adaptations (ad əp-tā′shənz) help protect them. Adaptations are behaviors or parts of living things that help the living things survive in their environment.

▲ **Sharp thorns of musk thistle**

▲ **Poison ivy leaves grow in threes.**

Quills and thorns are adaptations. Just as porcupines protect themselves with quills, some plants protect themselves with thorns. Thorns seem to say, "Stay away!"

Some plants, such as poison ivy, produce chemicals that protect them. Poison ivy can cause an itchy rash on someone who handles the plant. Mature milkweed plants are harmful for cattle and sheep to eat.

Protecting the life cycle of a plant protects the species. Species that can't protect themselves may die out. ■

INVESTIGATION 4

1. Scientists have put experiments on the space shuttle to see how plants grow in a weightless environment. How would roots and stems be affected? Predict some problems in growing seeds in space.

2. Explain one change in a plant's environment that can cause a growth change in the plant.

REFLECT & EVALUATE

WORD POWER

cone	pollen
embryo	pollination
fruit	scale
germinate	seed coat
petal	seedling
pistil	stamen

 On Your Own
Review the terms in the list. Then use as many terms as you can in a paragraph abut the life cycle of the plant.

With a Partner
Make up a quiz, using all the terms in the list. Challenge your partner to complete the quiz.

BUILD YOUR PORTFOLIO

Design your own seed catalog. List as many different kinds of seeds as you can. On each page of your catalog, draw and label a kind of seed. Include a picture of what the adult plant might look like.

Analyze Information

On a separate sheet of paper, make a larger copy of this drawing of a flower.
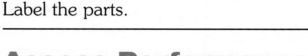
Use crayons or colored pencils to shade in these flower parts with the colors indicated: pistil—orange, stamen—blue, and petals—red. Label the parts.

Assess Performance

Use what you know about seeds to learn about peanuts. Study a peanut in its shell. Start by examining the outside of the peanut shell. Then carefully pull the shell apart to examine the seeds inside. Make a labeled diagram to show the seed coat and stored food.

Problem Solving

1. If the conifers in a forest did not produce cones one year, how would their life cycle be affected?

2. Fall has arrived, so you decide to clear out the dead pansy plants in your garden. The next spring you notice pansies growing in the garden. How did they get there?

3. In the park you notice squirrels collecting nuts, children picking flowers, bees buzzing around, and a bird building its nest. Explain which activities might help plant pollination.

Throughout this unit you've investigated questions related to life cycles, growth, and change. How will you use what you've learned and share that information with others? Here are some ideas.

Hold a Big Event
to Share Your Unit Project

With your classmates, plan a classroom book fair to share the Plant-Sitter's and Animal-Sitter's Guides that you have made. With your teacher's permission, you might invite other classes or adult friends and parents to the fair. If possible, offer copies of the guides to interested visitors.

Experiment

Plan a long-term project based on an activity in this unit. You might plant a flower or vegetable seed and observe as it changes from seed to seedling to a grown plant. You could measure the changes in its size, record them on a line graph, and then draw pictures to show other changes. You could also catch a caterpillar and watch as it changes into a pupa. You would have to make sure to provide it with the same food it eats in the wild. Or you might have another idea. Show your plan to your teacher before you begin.

Research

Find out how you've grown and changed since you were born. How have your height, weight, hair, and teeth changed? How have your writing and artwork changed? What toys did you like as a baby? What toys do you play with now? Report your findings in a booklet or poster about yourself. Make drawings or include photographs of yourself at different ages.

SCIENCE Handbook

You don't have to be a professional scientist to act and think like one. Thinking like a scientist mostly means using common sense. It also means learning how to test your ideas in a careful way.

In other words, *you* can think like a scientist.

Make a Hypothesis

Plan and Do a Test

Make Observations

To think like a scientist, you should learn as much as you can by observing things around you. Everything you hear and see is a clue about how the world works.

Ask a Question

Look for patterns. You'll get ideas and ask questions like these.

- Does a dripping faucet waste a lot of water?

- How does the time that the Sun sets change from day to day?

Make a Guess Called a Hypothesis

If you have an idea about why something happens, make an educated guess, or hypothesis, that you can test. For example, let's

suppose that your hypothesis about sunset time is that it changes by one minute each day.

Plan and Do a Test

Plan how to test your hypothesis. Your plan would need to consider some of these problems.

- How will you measure the time that the Sun sets?

- Will you measure the time every day?

- For how many days or weeks do you need to measure?

Record and Analyze What Happens

When you test your idea, you need to observe carefully and write down, or record, everything that

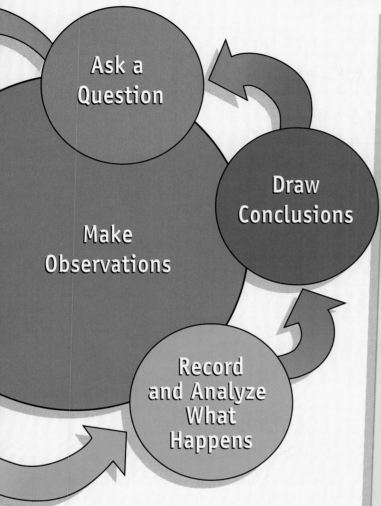

Ask a
Question

Draw
Conclusions

Make
Observations

Record
and Analyze
What
Happens

To think like a scientist, you need to practice certain ways of thinking.

Always check for yourself.
Ask, "How do I know it's true?" Be willing to find out for yourself.

Be honest and careful about what you observe.
It's easy to only look for the results you expect. It's harder to see the unexpected. But unexpected results lead scientists to ask more questions. They also provide information on how things work.

Don't be afraid to be wrong.
Based on their observations, scientists make many hypotheses. Not all of these hypotheses turn out to be correct. But scientists can learn from wrong "guesses," because even wrong guesses result in information that leads to knowledge.

Keep an open mind about possible explanations.
Make sure to think about all the reasons why something might have happened. Consider all the explanations that you can think of.

happens. When you finish collecting data, you may need to do some calculations with it. For example, you might calculate how much the sunset time changes in a week.

Draw Conclusions

Whatever happens in a test, think about all the reasons for your results. Sometimes this thinking leads to a new hypothesis.

If the time of the sunset changes by one minute each day, think about what else the data shows you. Can you predict the time that the Sun will set one month from now?

DOES A DRIPPING FAUCET WASTE A LOT OF WATER?

Here's an example of an everyday problem and how thinking like a scientist can help you explore it.

Nan's class is learning about saving water. Nan knows saving water is important, so she's surprised when she sees a dripping faucet. Nan showed the dripping faucet to her friend Carlos. He thinks such a little drip won't waste much water. "But it drips all the time," thinks Nan. "All the little drips may add up to a lot of water."

Make Observations

Ask a Question

Nan and Carlos wanted to find out more about the dripping faucet. They brainstormed questions that they wanted to answer.

• Does the dripping faucet waste water?

• How much water is lost by the dripping faucet?

Nan and Carlos decided to focus on the second question since they knew they could measure how much water was dripping. They were not sure what the answer would be. But they thought it was a good question to answer.

Scientific investigations often begin by thinking about what you already know. This can lead you to discover some ideas that you're not sure about and it can help you ask a question you want to answer.

Make a Hypothesis

Make Observations

Nan and Carlos watched the dripping faucet. They started counting the number of drips that fell in one minute. But they couldn't decide what was a little or what was a lot of water based on drips.

Nan suggested they measure how much water dripped out of the faucet in six hours. She also thought they should decide how much "a lot" was. They agreed to test the statement that the faucet drips 250 mL (1 c) of water in 6 hours. They decided that more than 250 mL would be "a lot." This statement was their hypothesis. A hypothesis is a possible answer to a question.

When you use what you've observed to suggest a possible answer to your question, you are making a hypothesis. If you can't think of an experiment or make a model to test your hypothesis, try changing it to something simpler and easier to test.

Make Observations

Plan and Do a Test

Carlos and Nan worked together and planned a way to test their hypothesis. They would need a container to catch all of the dripping water from the faucet. So Carlos asked Ms. Webb, their teacher, for a beaker that would hold at least 1,000 mL of water. The beaker that Mrs. Webb gave them had lines drawn on it. The lines showed, in milliliters, how much material the beaker could hold.

At 9:00 A.M., Carlos and Nan put the beaker under the dripping faucet. They made sure the water dripped directly into the beaker.

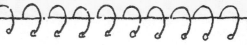

One way to try out your hypothesis is to use a test called an experiment. When you plan an experiment, make sure that it helps you to answer your question. Try to imagine what might happen when you do your experiment. Sometimes things happen that make the experiment not work properly. If the experiment doesn't work, you can change the plan for your experiment and try again.

Make Observations

Record and Analyze What Happened

Nan and Carlos checked the beaker every hour. Each hour, they recorded the time and the amount of water in the beaker. By 3:00 P.M., Nan and Carlos were very surprised by their findings. After 6 hours, the beaker had 1,500 mL of water in it!

They made a pictograph, like the one above, of what they observed.

When you do an experiment, you need to write down, or record, your observations and data. Then you need to organize your data in a way that helps you understand it. Then you analyze the data to learn what it tells you about your hypothesis.

MEASURING DRIPS

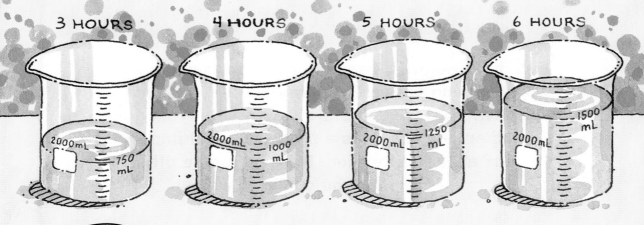

3 HOURS — 750 mL (2000mL)

4 HOURS — 1000 mL (2000mL)

5 HOURS — 1250 mL (2000mL)

6 HOURS — 1500 mL (2000mL)

Make Observations

Draw Conclusions

Nan and Carlos told their class about the results of their experiment. Everyone agreed that dripping faucets waste a lot of water. But they still had questions.

Do all dripping faucets waste this much water?

Do only faucets drip, or do water pipes drip, too?

If a little drip adds up to so much water, how much water do we use in everyday activities?

The students decided to plan experiments to find out the answers to their questions. Carlos and Nan decided to carry their experiment further. They decided to find out how much water the dripping faucet wastes in 24 hours.

After you have analyzed your data, you should use what you have learned to draw a conclusion. A conclusion is a statement that sums up what you have learned. Think about whether or not the information you have gathered supports your hypothesis. If it does, figure out how to explore your idea more thoroughly. But always think about the new questions you can ask from what you've discovered.

SAFETY

The best way to be safe in the classroom is to use common sense. Prepare yourself for each activity before you start it. Get help from your teacher when there is a problem. Most important of all, pay attention. Here are some other ways that you can stay safe.

Stay Safe From Stains

- Wear protective clothing or an old shirt when you work with messy materials.
- If anything spills, wipe it up or ask your teacher to help you clean it up.

Stay Safe From Injuries

- Protect your eyes by wearing safety goggles when you are told that you need them.
- Keep your hands dry around electricity. Water is a good conductor of electricity, so you can get a shock more easily if your hands are wet.
- Be careful with sharp objects. If you have to press on them, keep the sharp side away from you.
- Cover any cuts you have that are exposed. If you spill something on a cut, be sure to wash it off immediately.
- Don't eat or drink anything unless your teacher tells you that it's okay.

Stay Safe From Flames

- Keep your clothes away from open flames. If you have long or baggy sleeves, roll them up.
- Don't let your hair get close to a flame. If you have long hair, tie it back.

Stay Safe During Cleanup

- Wash up after you finish working.
- Dispose of things in the way that your teacher tells you to.

MOST IMPORTANTLY

If you ever hurt yourself or one of your group members gets hurt, tell your teacher right away.

HAIR Keep it out of the way of a flame.

EYES Wear safety goggles when you are told to.

CLOTHES Keep long sleeves rolled up. Protect yourself from stains. Stay away from open flames.

DON'T MAKE A MESS If you spill something, clean it up right away. When finished with an activity, clean up your work area. Dispose of things in the way your teacher tells you to.

MOUTH Don't eat or drink ANYTHING unless your teacher tells you it's okay.

HANDS Keep your hands dry around electricity. Cover any cuts. Wear gloves when told to. Wash up after you finish.

Using a
Hand Lens

A hand lens is a tool that magnifies objects, or makes objects appear larger. This makes it possible for you to see details of an object that would be hard to see without the hand lens.

▲ **Place the lens above the object.**

Look at a Coin or a Stamp

1. Place an object such as a coin or a stamp on a table or other flat surface.

2. Hold the hand lens just above the object. As you look through the lens, slowly move the lens away from the object. Notice that the object appears to get larger.

3. Keep moving the lens until the object begins to look a little blurry. Then move the hand lens a little closer to the object until the object is once again in sharp focus.

▲ Move the lens slowly toward you.

If the object becomes blurry, you need to move the lens toward the object. ▶

Using a Calculator

After you've made measurements, a calculator can help you analyze your data. Some calculators have a memory key that allows you to save the result of one calculation while you do another.

Find an Average

The table shows the amount of rain that fell each month of one year. Use a calculator to find the average monthly rainfall.

1. To add the numbers, enter a number and then press the plus sign (+). Repeat until you enter the last number. Then press the equal sign (=).

2. If you make a mistake, push the clear entry key (CE). Enter the number again, and then continue adding.

3. Your total should be 1,131. You can use the total to find the average. Just press divide (÷) and enter 12, the number of months in a year.

4. Your answer should be 94.25.

Rainfall	
Month	Rain (mm)
Jan.	214
Feb.	138
Mar.	98
Apr.	157
May	84
June	41
July	5
Aug.	23
Sept.	48
Oct.	75
Nov.	140
Dec.	108

clear entry

divide

equal

plus

Using a Balance

A balance is used to measure mass. Mass is the amount of matter in an object. Place the object to be massed in the left pan of the balance. Place standard masses in the right pan.

Measure the Mass of an Orange

1. Check that the empty pans are balanced, or level with each other. When balanced, the pointer on the base should be at the middle mark. If it needs to be adjusted, move the slider on the back of the balance a little to the left or right.

2. Place an orange on the left pan. Then add standard masses, one at a time, to the right pan. When the pointer is at the middle mark again, each pan holds the same amount of matter and has the same mass.

3. Add the numbers marked on the masses in the pan. The total is the mass in grams of the orange.

Using a
Tape Measure or Ruler

Tape measures and rulers are tools for measuring the length of objects and distances. Scientists most often use units such as meters, centimeters, and millimeters when making length measurements.

Use a Tape Measure

1. Wrap the tape around the jar.

2. Find the line where the tape begins to wrap over itself.

3. Record the distance around the jar in centimeters.

Use a Metric Ruler

1. Place the ruler or the meterstick on the floor. Line up the end of the ruler with the heel of your shoe.

2. Notice where the other end of your shoe lines up with the ruler.

3. Look at the scale. Record the length of your shoe in centimeters and in millimeters.

Using a
Thermometer

A thermometer is used to measure temperature. When the liquid in the tube of a thermometer gets warmer, it expands and moves farther up the tube. Different scales can be used to measure temperature, but scientists usually use the Celsius scale.

Measure the Temperature of a Cold Liquid

1. Take a chilled liquid out of the refrigerator. Half-fill a cup with the liquid.

2. Hold the thermometer so that the bulb is in the center of the liquid. Be sure that there are no bright lights or direct sunlight shining on the bulb.

3. Wait a couple of minutes until you see the liquid in the tube stop moving. Read the scale line that is closest to the top of the liquid in the tube. The thermometer shown reads 4°C (40°F).

Measuring
Volume

A graduated cylinder, a measuring cup, and a beaker are used to measure volume. Volume is the amount of space something takes up. Most of the containers that scientists use to measure volume have a scale marked in milliliters (mL).

Measure the Volume of Juice

1. Pour the juice into a measuring container.

2. Move your head so that your eyes are level with the top of the juice. Read the scale line that is closest to the surface of the juice. If the surface of the juice is curved up on the sides, look at the lowest point of the curve.

3. Read the measurement on the scale. You can estimate the value between two lines on the scale.

▲ The bottom of the curve is at 35 mL.

◄ This graduated cylinder has marks for every 5 mL.

This beaker has marks for each 25 mL. ▼

▼ This measuring cup has marks for each 25 mL.

MEASUR

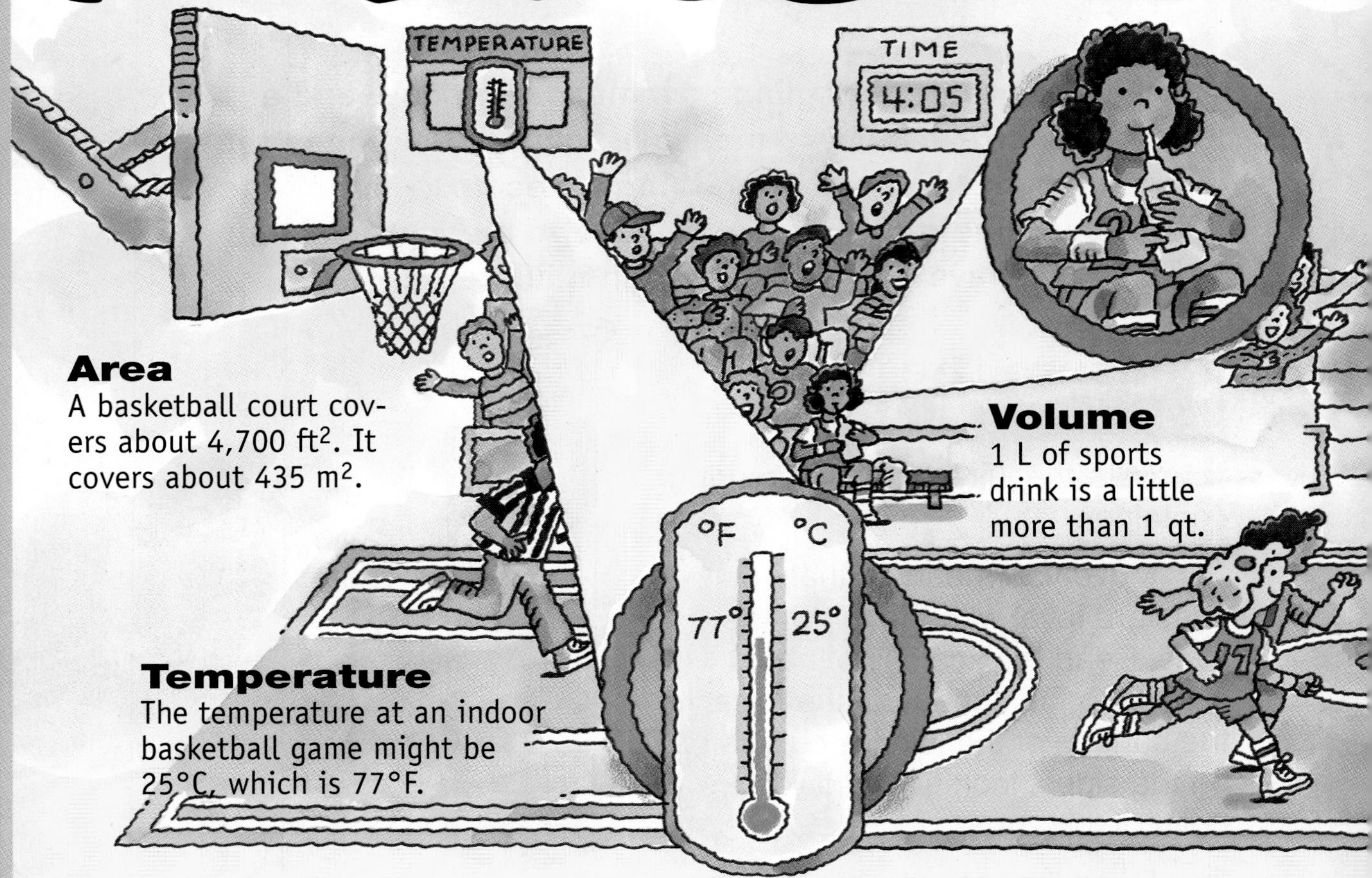

Area
A basketball court covers about 4,700 ft^2. It covers about 435 m^2.

TEMPERATURE

TIME 4:05

Volume
1 L of sports drink is a little more than 1 qt.

°F   °C

77°   25°

Temperature
The temperature at an indoor basketball game might be 25°C, which is 77°F.

SI Measures

Temperature
Ice melts at 0 degrees Celsius (°C)

Water freezes at 0°C

Water boils at 100°C

Length and Distance
1,000 meters (m) = 1 kilometer (km)

100 centimeters (cm) = 1 m

10 millimeters (mm) = 1 cm

Force
1 newton (N) =
1 kilogram x meter/second/second
(kg x m/s^2)

Volume
1 cubic meter (m^3) = 1 m x 1 m x 1 m

1 cubic centimeter (cm^3) =
1 cm x 1 cm x 1 cm

1 liter (L) = 1,000 milliliters (mL)

1 cm^3 = 1 mL

Area
1 square kilometer (km^2) = 1 km x 1 km

1 hectare = 10,000 m^2

Mass
1,000 grams (g) = 1 kilogram (kg)

1,000 milligrams (mg) = 1 g

EMENTS

Mass and Weight
A basketball has a mass of about 650 g. It weighs about $1\frac{1}{2}$ lb.

Length/Distance
A basketball rim is about 10 ft high, or a little more than 3 m from the floor.

Rates (SI and English)

km/h = kilometers per hour

m/s = meters per second

mph = miles per hour

English Measures

Volume of Fluids
8 fluid ounces (fl oz) = 1 cup (c)

2 c = 1 pint (pt)

2 pt = 1 quart (qt)

4 qt = 1 gallon (gal)

Temperature
Ice melts at 32 degrees Fahrenheit (°F)

Water freezes at 32°F

Water boils at 212°F

Length and Distance
12 inches (in.) = 1 foot (ft)

3 ft = 1 yard (yd)

5,280 ft = 1 mile (mi)

Weight
16 ounces (oz) = 1 pound (lb)   2,000 pounds = 1 ton (T)

GLOSSARY

Pronunciation Key

Symbol	Key Words
a	cat
ā	ape
ä	cot, car
e	ten, berry
ē	me
i	fit, here
ī	ice, fire
ō	go
ô	fall, for
oi	oil
o͞o	look, pull
o͞o	tool, rule
ou	out, crowd
u	up
ʉ	fur, shirt
ə	a in ago
	e in agent
	i in pencil
	o in atom
	u in circus
b	bed
d	dog
f	fall

Symbol	Key Words
g	get
h	help
j	jump
k	kiss, call
l	leg
m	meat
n	nose
p	put
r	red
s	see
t	top
v	vat
w	wish
y	yard
z	zebra
ch	chin, arch
ŋ	ring, drink
sh	she, push
th	thin, truth
th	then, father
zh	measure

A heavy stress mark ' is placed after a syllable that gets a heavy, or primary, stress, as in **picture** (pik′chər).

acid rain (as'id rān) Rain, containing a large amount of acids, that results from the burning of fossil fuels. (D56) *Acid rain* can harm living things.

adaptation (ad əp tā'shən) Behavior or part of a living thing that helps it survive in a certain environment. (E40) A rose's thorns and a camel's hump are *adaptations*.

air pollution (er pə l$\overline{oo}$'shən) Any harmful or unclean materials in the air. (C50) Burning fuels can cause *air pollution*.

aquifer (ak'wə fər) Underground layers of soil, sand, or gravel that store ground water. (D27) The water in a well usually comes from an *aquifer*.

astronomer (ə strän'ə mər) A scientist who studies the origin, features, and motion of objects in space. (B14) *Astronomers* use telescopes, cameras, and space probes to study the stars.

atmosphere (at'məs fir) The layer of gases surrounding Earth or another planet. (B12) Earth's *atmosphere* is made up of gases such as oxygen.

axis (ak'sis) The imaginary line on which an object rotates. (B38) Earth's *axis* runs between the North Pole and the South Pole.

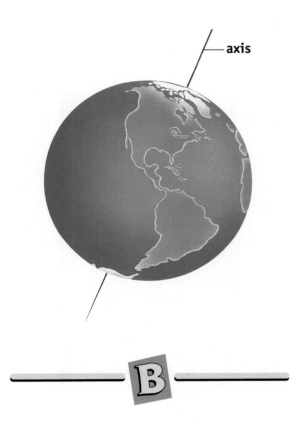

axis

bacteria (bak tir'ē ə) Tiny living things that can cause illness. (F36) Some *bacteria* cause diseases, such as tetanus and strep, but others are helpful to the body.

behavior (bē hāv'yər) The way an animal usually acts in a certain situation. (E42) One *behavior* of pill bugs is to move toward moist, dark places.

C

camouflage (kam′ə fläzh) The ability to blend in with the surroundings. (E45) An animal's fur or skin can be *camouflage*, helping the animal hunt or avoid hunters.

carbohydrates (kär bō hī′drāts) Food sugars and starches that are used by the body for energy. (F11) Potatoes, noodles, apples, and cereals all contain *carbohydrates*.

carnivore (kär′nə vôr) An animal that eats only other animals. (E17) Wolves, cougars, lions, hawks, and owls are *carnivores*.

cell (sel) The tiny unit that makes up all living things. (F44) Each *cell* can grow, respond, reproduce, and use energy, yet all your cells work together to keep you alive.

chyme (kīm) A thick, souplike mixture of food and digestive juices. (F59) *Chyme* forms as the stomach digests food.

community (kə myo͞o′nə tē) A group of plants and animals that live in a certain area. (E31) A pond's plants and animals form a *community*.

complete metamorphosis (kəm plēt′ met ə môr′fə sis) The four-stage life cycle of some insects. (A25) A life cycle that goes from egg to larva to pupa to adult is described as a *complete metamorphosis*.

condense (kən dens′) To change form from a gas to a liquid. (C43, D16) When water vapor in the air cools, it *condenses* into tiny droplets of liquid water.

conduction (kən duk′shən) The transfer of heat through direct contact between particles of matter. (C35) Heat moves by *conduction* from warmer matter with faster-moving particles to cooler matter with slower-moving particles.

conductor (kən duk′tər) A type of material that transfers heat or electricity. (C36) Metals are good *conductors* of heat.

cone (kōn) The part of a conifer that produces pollen or seeds. (A52) Each *cone* is a woody stalk covered with stiff scales.

constellation (kän stə lā'shən) A group of stars that form a pattern that looks like a person, animal, or object. (B47) Different *constellations* are visible from Earth at different times of year.

consumer (kən soom'ər) A living thing that eats other living things to survive. (E16) Animals are *consumers*.

convection (kən vek'shən) The circulation of heat through a liquid or gas (fluid). (C36) *Convection* takes place in a room with a heater: As hot air rises from the heater, cool air flows down to take its place.

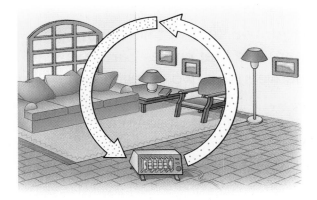

crater (krāt'ər) A bowl-shaped pit. (B11) *Craters* on the Moon and on Earth were formed by meteorites striking the surface.

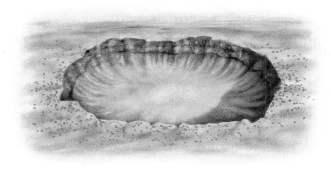

current (kʉr'ənt) A stream of water or air. (D67) The hot-air balloon rode a *current* of air as it moved toward the mountains.

decomposer (dē kəm pōz'ər) A living thing that breaks down and feeds on the remains of once-living things. (E18) *Decomposers* such as mushrooms recycle the remains of once-living things.

digestion (di jes'chən) The process of breaking down food into a form that can be used by the body's cells. (F44) The body breaks down food by physical and chemical *digestion*.

dissolve (di zälv′) To mix or cause to mix one material, usually a solid, in another material, often a liquid, so that both materials separate into tiny particles that can't be seen. (D44) Sugar *dissolves* rapidly in hot water.

distilled water (di stild′ wôt′ər) Water that does not contain minerals, chemicals, or air. (D44) *Distilled water* is pure water.

egg (eg) The first stage in the life cycle of almost all animals. (A14) Birds hatch from *eggs* outside the mother bird's body.

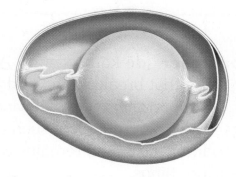

embryo (em′brē ō) An animal or plant in the *earliest* stages of its development. (A15, A41) A plant *embryo* is the tiny plant that is found inside a seed.

energy (en′ər jē) The ability to move something or cause a change in matter. (C11) A car uses *energy* from gasoline to run.

energy of motion (en′ər jē uv mō′shən) The energy that moving matter has. (C11) Sliding downhill on a sled, tossing a basketball into the air, and flying a kite in the wind are examples of *energy of motion*.

environment (en vī′rən mənt) All the surrounding living and non-living things that affect a living thing. (E10) A drop of water, a rotting log, a desert, the ocean, and a rain forest are examples of different *environments*.

enzymes (en′zīmz) Chemicals in the body, some of which help speed up the process of digestion. (F59) Digestive *enzymes* in the stomach help the breakdown of food in the body.

equator (ē kwā′tər) An imaginary line that circles Earth halfway between the two poles. (B64) If you live near the *equator,* you live in a hot climate because your region receives direct sunlight year-round.

esophagus (i säf′ə gəs) The muscular tube that connects the mouth to the stomach. (F47) After you swallow food, it travels through the *esophagus* to the stomach.

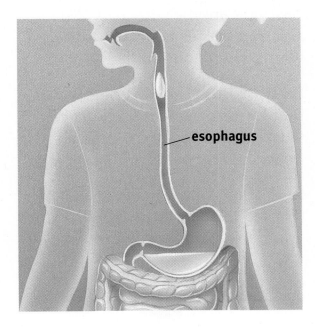

— esophagus

evaporate (ē vap′ə rāt) To change form from a liquid to a gas. (C42, D15) On a warm dry day, water puddles on the sidewalk *evaporate* quickly.

extinction (ek stiŋk′shən) The permanent disappearance of all living things of a certain kind. (E31) The dinosaurs' *extinction* is a mystery that many scientists are working to solve.

fats (fats) High-energy nutrients that are oily or greasy. (F11) Cheeses, meats, nuts, and butter are foods that are usually high in *fats*.

fiber (fī′bər) Strands of plant material that are indigestible. (F61) Although *fiber* can't be digested, it aids in the process of digestion.

flare (fler) A bright area on the surface of the Sun caused by a solar storm. (B27) A solar *flare* is hotter than surrounding areas of the Sun and so is brighter.

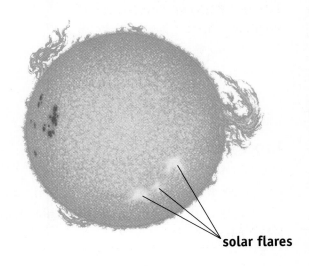

solar flares

food chain (fōōd chān) The path that energy takes through a community as one living thing eats another. (E26) The first link in a *food chain* is usually a plant.

food web (fōōd web) Two or more overlapping food chains. (E28) A *food web* connects animals through the plants and animals that they eat.

fossil fuel (fäs′əl fyōō′əl) A fuel formed over time from the remains of plants or animals. (C50) *Fossil fuels* such as oil, coal, and natural gas are found underground.

freeze (frēz) To change form from a liquid to a solid. (C43) The loss of heat causes a liquid to *freeze*.

friction (frik′shən) A force that keeps two objects from moving past one another easily. (C29) *Friction* causes your hands to get warm when you rub them together.

fruit (frōōt) The part of a flower that forms around a seed. (A47) Cucumbers, tomatoes, oranges, peaches, and pears are *fruits*.

fuel (fyōō′əl) A material that can be used for energy. (C50) Wood is a *fuel* used in many countries.

gas (gas) A state of matter that has no definite shape and does not take up a definite amount of space. (D14) A *gas* spreads out evenly to fill whatever space it is in.

germ (jʉrm) A tiny organism that can cause disease. (D49) Chlorine kills some of the *germs* in water.

germinate (jʉr′mə nāt) To sprout and begin to develop into a seedling. (A42) Most kinds of seeds need moisture, air, and warmth to *germinate*.

gravity (grav′i tē) A force that pulls two or more objects toward each other. (B22, D36) To fly into space, a rocket must overcome Earth's *gravity*.

ground water (ground wôt′ər) The water found beneath Earth's surface. (D27) In some areas, *ground water* fills the small spaces that are between underground rocks, soil, and sand.

hard water (härd wôt′ər) Water in which large amounts of minerals are dissolved. (D44) The minerals in *hard water* can stain clothing and give water an unpleasant taste.

healthful diet (helth′fəl dī′ət) A diet made up of a variety of foods that supply all necessary nutrients. (F18) A *healthful diet* is one that is high in fruits, vegetables, and cereals and low in fats and sweets.

heat (hēt) The energy of moving particles of matter. (C12) Adding *heat* to matter causes its particles to move faster.

herbivore (hʉr′bə vôr) An animal that eats only plants. (E18) Cows, butterflies, mice, and rabbits are *herbivores*.

hibernation (hī bər nā′shən) A deep sleep that helps some animals survive the winter. (E77) An animal that is in *hibernation* breathes more slowly, has a slower heartbeat, and has a lower body temperature.

incomplete metamorphosis (in kəm plēt′ met ə môr′fə sis) The three-stage life cycle of some insects. (A26) A life cycle that goes from egg to nymph to adult is described as an *incomplete metamorphosis*.

H25

insulator (in′sə lā tər) A poor conductor of heat or electricity. (C36) Air that is trapped in the small spaces between fibers of clothing acts as an *insulator*.

junk food (juŋk fo͞od) A food low in nutrients and high in fat, sugar, or salt. (F30) Candy, potato chips, and soda are *junk foods*.

large intestine (lärj in tes′tən) The digestive organ that stores waste and absorbs water from it. (F61) The major job of the *large intestine* is to absorb water from wastes and return it to the blood-stream.

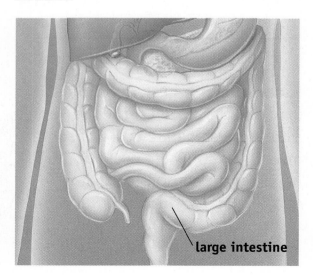

large intestine

larva (lär′və) The second stage in the life cycle of an insect that undergoes complete metamorphosis. (A25) A butterfly *larva* is called a caterpillar.

life cycle (līf sī′kəl) The series of changes that occur during the lifetime of a living thing. (A9) An insect goes through three or four stages in its *life cycle*.

liquid (lik′wid) A state of matter that has no definite shape but takes up a definite amount of space. (D14) At room temperature, water is a *liquid*.

lunar eclipse (lo͞o′nər i klips′) The darkening of the Moon when it moves into Earth's shadow. (B78) During a *lunar eclipse*, Earth blocks the Sun's light from reaching the Moon directly.

matter (mat'ər) Anything that has mass and takes up space. (C11) Every living and nonliving thing around you is made of *matter*.

melt (melt) To change form from a solid to a liquid. (C42) Ice *melts* at 0°C (32°F) or warmer.

meteorite (mēt'ē ər īt) A chunk of rock or metal that has fallen from space. (B11) A *meteorite* may be as small as a grain of sand or as large as a house.

migrate (mī'grāt) To move to another region as the seasons change. (E76) Many northern birds and butterflies *migrate* south during the winter.

minerals (min'ər əlz) Chemicals that can be important nutrients. (F13) Calcium is a *mineral* found in milk and cheese.

natural resource (nach'ər əl rē'sôrs) A material found in or on Earth that people use. (D10) *Natural resources* include water, minerals, oil, plants, and animals.

nutrient (nōō'trē ənt) Any substance used by living things for energy, growth, repair, or other life processes. (E43, F10) Proteins, carbohydrates, and fats are *nutrients* found in food.

nymph (nimf) The second stage in the life cycle of an insect undergoing incomplete metamorphosis. (A26) A grasshopper *nymph* looks similar to a small adult.

omnivore (äm'ni vôr) An animal that eats both plants and animals. (E18) Because bears will eat both berries and fish, bears are classified as *omnivores*.

orbit (ôr'bit) The path a planet, moon, or other object takes around another. (B47) The Moon is seen in different phases as it moves through its *orbit* around Earth.

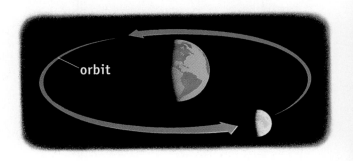

orbit

palate (pal'ət) The roof of the mouth. (F45) During the first part of digestion, the tongue mashes food against the *palate*.

parasite (par'ə sīt) A living thing that, at some point in its life, lives on or in another living thing. (E54) Fleas and lice are *parasites*.

petal (pet''l) The brightly colored part of a flower that helps attract birds, bees, and other insects to the flower. (A46) A *petal* is one of the three main parts of a flower.

phase (fāz) Any stage in the series of changes in the apparent shape of the Moon. (B53) The Moon's shape appears to change with each *phase*.

pistil (pis'til) The central part in a flower that produces the seed. (A45) For seeds to form in a plant, the pollen must travel to the *pistil*.

planet (plan'it) Any large body that orbits a star and does not produce light of its own. (B47) Earth is a *planet*.

plaque (plak) The coating produced by bacteria on uncleaned teeth. (F51) *Plaque* is caused by bacteria in the mouth.

pollen (päl'ən) The powdery grains in a flower; they must be carried from a stamen to a pistil in order for seeds to form. (A46) Bees move *pollen* from one flower to another.

pollination (päl ə nā'shən) The process by which pollen reaches a pistil. (A46) After *pollination*, a flower can produce seeds.

polluted (pə lo͞ot'əd) Containing unwanted or harmful material. (D58) Breathing *polluted* air can be harmful to your lungs.

precipitation (prē sip ə tā'shən) The liquid or solid forms of water that fall to Earth. (D16) Rain, sleet, hail, and snow are different kinds of *precipitation*.

predator (pred'ə tər) An animal that hunts other animals for food. (E27) Hawks, cougars, and sharks are *predators*.

prey (prā) An animal hunted for food by another animal. (E27) Rabbits, mice, small fish, and insects are often *prey* for other, larger animals.

producer (prō dōōs'ər) A living thing that can make its own food. (E16) Plants, such as trees and grass, are *producers*.

prominence (präm'ə nəns) A huge loop of gas that appears on the edge of the Sun. (B27) *Prominences* are caused by magnetic storms on the Sun.

proteins (prō'tēnz) Nutrients used by the body for growth and repair. (F12) *Proteins* are found in foods such as meats, beans, nuts, and dairy products.

pupa (pyōō'pə) The third stage in the life cycle of an insect undergoing complete metamorphosis. (A25) As a *pupa*, an insect is enclosed in a cocoon, or case.

— R —

radiation (rā dē ā'shən) The movement of heat energy in the form of waves. (C37) Heat from a campfire reaches you through *radiation*.

reservoir (rez'ər vwär) The body of water that is stored behind a dam. (D27) A *reservoir* stores fresh water for a town or city.

revolve (ri välv') To move in a circle or orbit. (B47) Earth *revolves* around the Sun.

rotation (rō tā'shən) Turning around an axis. (B38) Earth takes 24 hours to complete one *rotation*.

saliva (sə lī′və) The watery liquid, secreted into the mouth, that aids in chewing, swallowing, and digesting. (F46) *Saliva* moistens food, making it easier to swallow the food.

salivary glands (sal′ə ver ē glandz) Small organs that make saliva. (F46) The *salivary glands* are found under the jaw, under the tongue, and next to the ears.

scale (skāl) A cone's woody part on which seeds grow. (A51, A53) A pine cone's *scales* protect its seeds.

season (sē′zən) Any of the four parts of the year. (B65) The four *seasons* are spring, summer, fall, and winter.

seed coat (sēd kōt) The part of a seed that protects the plant embryo. (A41) The *seed coat* of a coconut is hard, thick, and brown.

seedling (sēd′liŋ) The new plant that develops from an embryo and has roots, a stem, and leaves. (A43) A tomato *seedling* can be started indoors in early spring and planted outside in May.

small intestine (smôl in tes′tən) The long, coiled organ in which most digestion takes place. (F60) Nutrients in food are absorbed into the bloodstream from the *small intestine*.

soft water (sôft wôt′ər) Water in which few minerals are dissolved. (D44) Minerals can be removed from water to make *soft water*.

solar eclipse (sō′lər i klips′) The blocking of light from the Sun when the Moon moves between it and Earth. (B77) During a *solar eclipse*, the Sun's light is blocked by the Moon.

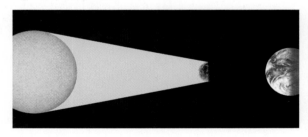

solar energy (sō′lər en′ər jē) Energy produced by the Sun. (C20) *Solar energy* can be used to produce electricity.

solar system (sō′lər sis′təm) The Sun and all the planets and other objects that orbit it. (B47) Earth is one of nine planets in the *solar system*.

solid (säl′id) A state of matter that has a definite shape and takes up a definite amount of space. (D14) A rock, a piece of ice, and a chair are all examples of *solids*.

species (spē′shēz) A group of living things that can produce young by mating with one another. (A10) The lion *species* cannot produce young of the gorilla *species*.

stamen (stā′mən) The part of a flower that produces pollen, which is needed to form seeds. (A45) *Stamens* are often long and have a fuzzy end.

star (stär) A ball of very hot gases that gives off light and other kinds of energy. (B27) The Sun is a *star*.

stomach (stum′ək) A muscular sac that stores food and helps in digestion. (F59) The *stomach* squeezes and churns food into a souplike mixture.

stored energy (stôrd en′ər jē) Energy that can cause matter to move or change. (C11) Fuels have *stored energy* from the Sun.

sunspot (sun′spöt) A dark area on the surface of the Sun, caused by a solar storm. (B27) A *sunspot* appears darker because it is cooler than surrounding areas of the Sun.

surface water (sur′fis wôt′ər) Fresh water in lakes, streams, and rivers. (D26) People often pipe *surface water* to nearby cities and towns.

telescope (tel′ə skōp) An instrument that makes distant objects appear nearer and larger. (B14) A *telescope* is used to study stars and other planets.

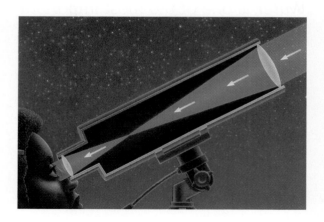

temperature (tem′pər ə chər) How hot or cold something is. (C28) *Temperature* is measured with a thermometer.

tide (tīd) The rise and fall of the ocean surface, mostly caused by the pull of the Moon's gravity. (D68) Along coasts, there are two high *tides* and two low *tides* during each day.

vitamins (vīt'ə minz) Chemicals, found in foods, that are important nutrients. (F13) *Vitamins* do not supply energy, but they are important to many body processes.

water (wôt'ər) A chemical, formed from hydrogen and oxygen, that is essential to life. (F12) *Water* is one of the most important nutrients.

water cycle (wôt'ər sī'kəl) The path that water follows from Earth to air and back again. (D16) In the *water cycle*, water evaporates from lakes and oceans into the air, and then condenses and falls back to Earth as rain or snow.

water pressure (wôt'ər presh'ər) The pushing of water on a surface. (D36) The deeper the water, the greater the *water pressure* becomes.

water vapor (wôt'ər vā'pər) Water that is a gas. (D15) Steam, which is invisible, is a form of *water vapor*.

INDEX

A

Acid
  in mouth, F51
  in stomach, F59
Acid rain, D56–D57*, D59, D62
Adaptation, A42, A60, A62, E36, E38*, E40. *See also* Behavior of animals; Camouflage; Protection.
  in animals, E40–E43, E54–E55
  to environment, E70*, E72, E74–E75
  in plants, A60–A62, E43
Adult, A9, A24–A27
Air, A43, A54, B12–B13, C18, C33*, C37–C38, D10, D15, D49, F62
Alaska
  midnight sun, B71
Animals, A6–A7*, A8–A9, A10–A11, A42, A48, A55, B28, D69, D70
  baby animals, A10, A18, A28–A29*
  claws, E40
  eggs, A14, A16, A18
  fangs, E40
  growth and change, A20–A21*
  life cycle, A12–A13*
  senses, E40
  tongues, E40, E41, E44–E45
  use of tools, E42–E43
Annuals (flowers), A48
Aquifer, D27–D28, D61
  Ogalalla Aquifer, D61
Arctic tern, E76
Aryabhata I, B48
Astronaut, B21, B23, B30
  Aldrin, Buzz, B23

Armstrong, Neil, B23
Astronomer, B14, B29
Atmosphere, B12
  on Earth, B12
  on Moon, B13
Axis, B38–B39, B65

B

Bacteria, D49, D51, E13, F34–F35, F36–F37, F51, F53, F62. *See also* Germs.
  needs of, E13
Beavers, E64–E65
Beetles, E73
Behavior of animals, E42, E52–E54
  as adaptation, E42
  as protection, E52–E54
  stalking of prey, E43
Binoculars, B15
Birds, A8, A42, A45, A47, A48, A55, A62, C38, E38–E39*, E55, E67, E76
  beaks (bills), E38–E39*, E41–E42
  feathers, C38
  water birds, E64
Birdseye, Clarence, F35
Blood, F12
Bloodstream, F44, F60
Blood vessels, F61
Body, F10, F12, F18, F44, F56
  growth, F10, F12, F18, F31
  repair, F10, F12, F18
Bog, E66
Bones, F13
Breathing, F12
Buffaloes (bison), E68–E69
  Wood Buffalo Park, E69

Bulb (plant), A41, A43
Burning (a way of changing matter), C44
Bush, A54
Butterfly, A25

C

Cactus, A60, E75
Calendars, B67–B69
  of Caesar, B68–B69
  Chinese, B68
  Greenwich, England, B69
  Mayan, B67
  Roman, B68–B69
Calories, F26–F27*, F28, F30
Camouflage, E45
  in animals, E50
  in chameleons, E45
  in insects, E48–E49*
Canning (to keep food fresh), F35
Car, C4, C11, C12, C18
Carbohydrates, F10–F11, F13, F18–F20, F28–F29, F59. *See also* Starches; Sugar.
Carbon dioxide, A16
Caries, F51
Carnivores, E17
Caterpillar, A25, A62
Cell, F44, F61
Chemicals, D43, D45, D59, D60, D71. *See also* Enzymes.
  in small intestine, F60
  in stomach, F59
Chesapeake Bay, D70–D71
Chewing, F45–F46
Chlorine (in water), D43, D50–D51
Cholesterol, F26–F27*, F28
Chyme, F59

chemical energy, C13,
C14*, C17, C18, C19
electrical energy, C12,
C19, C24*
energy and motion,
C8–C9*, C10, C11–C13
food energy, F10–F11,
F13, F18, F28–F29, F31,
F44
geothermal energy, C55
heat energy, C12, C14*,
C17, C18, C19, C24*,
C26*, C27, C35–C36,
C43, D15
light energy, C13, C14*,
C17, C18, C19, C20,
C37
mechanical energy, C12,
C18
nuclear energy, C53
radiant energy (radiation),
C37
saving energy, C56*,
C60–C62
solar energy, C4, C34*,
C37, C52
sound energy, C24–C25*
sources of energy, C50
stored energy, C11
water energy, C52
wind energy, C52
Environment, A42, A62,
D62–D63, E10, E40,
E42, E60, E62–E63*,
E65, E66–E67,
E70–E71*, E74–E76
changes in, E60,
E62–E63*, E65,
E66–E67, E76
pollution of. See Pollution.
Environmental Protection
Agency (EPA), D63, D71
Enzymes, F54–F55*, F59,
F60. See also Lactase.
Esophagus, F44, F46, F58
Estuary, D70

Evaporation, C42, D15,
D18–D19, D45
Everglades National Park,
E77
Evergreen, A52–A53
Extinction, E31
Eyes, F12

F
Factories, D62
Farmland, E69
Fats, F4, F8–F9*, F10–F11,
F13, F18–F20,
F26–F27*, F28, F30,
F59
saturated fat, F26–F27*,
F28
Feathers, C38, E70–E71*
Fertilizer, D54, D59, D71
Fiber
in cloth, C38
in foods, F4, F29,
F56–F57*, F61–F62
Fire, A54–A55
forest fire, A54
Fish, E42, E64, E67
Flower, A44–A45*,
A46–A48, A52
wildflowers, E65
Fluid, C36. See also Gas;
Liquid.
Fluorescent light, C61
Food, A11, A15, A20–A21*,
A22–A23*, A28–A29*,
A30, A31, A33–A34,
A40, A41, A43, C4,
C6*, C13, C18, E36,
E38–E39*, E40, E74,
E76, E78, F6–F7*,
F8–F9*, F14, F16–F17*,
F19–F20, F28,
F32–F33*, F40,
F42–F43*, F44–F45,
F50, F54–F55*,
F56–F57*
additives, F14

as fuel, F11. See also
Energy: food energy.
cleanness, F32–F33*,
F36–F37
groups, F18–F20
fortified, F15
freshness, F34
junk, F30–F31
labels, F15, F26–F27*, F28
poisoning, F38
serving size, F20, F28
Food chain, E22–E23*,
E24–E25*, E26–E29
Food energy. See Energy:
food energy.
Food Guide Pyramid,
F18–F20, F22
Food web, E24–E25*,
E28–E29
Fossil fuels, C50–C51, C58,
C60–C61
coal, C13, C18, C51–C52,
C58
natural gas, C51, C58
oil, C13, C18, C51, C58
uses, C51
Freezing, C43–C44, D15,
D38
Friction, C26*, C29
Frogs, E64
Fruit, A46, A49, F20, F30
Fuel, C11, C13, C18, C50

G
Gallbladder, F60
Gas, C27–C28, C33*, C36,
C42–C43, D14, D17
Gasoline, C11, C18
as pollutant, D59, D62
Germinate, A43, A55
Germs, D43, D49,
F32–F33*. See also
Bacteria.
Glucose, F54–F55*
test strip, F54–F55*
Grass, E65, E67

Medicines, from nature,
E56–E58
Melting, C42
Metamorphosis
complete, A25–A25
incomplete, A26
Meteor, B4
Meteorite, B11–B12
Microscope, B12, D50
Microwave oven, C27
Microwaves, C29
Migration, E76, E78
Minerals (in diet), F10, F13,
F14, F18–F19, F28–F29
Moisture, A42, A43,
A50–A51*, A53, A54,
E72–E74
Molds, E15
Moon, B4, B6–B7*, B8–B9*,
B10–B11, B14,
B16–B17, B18–B19*,
B20, B52–B55, D68
air, B13
atmosphere, B13
craters, B8–B9*, B11–B12
effects on Earth, B56
gravity, B23, B56
mass, B22
mountains, B11
new moon, B54
phases, B50–B51*, B53
plains, B11
revolution, B52–B53
rock as part of, B10–B11,
B22
Sea of Tranquillity, B11
size, B6–B7*
sky of, B13
soil as part of, B10, B16,
B23
temperature, B13
valleys, B11
water, B13
Motion, C8–C9*
Mucus, F59
Muscles, F12, F45, F47,
F58–F62

N

Natural resources, D10, D61
Nectar, A47
Needles (of plants), A52
Neighborhood, E62–E63*
Night, E74, E76
North Pole, B14, B38, B40
North Star, B40. *See also*
Constellations: Polaris.
Northern Hemisphere, B65
Northern lights, B29
Nose, F42–F43*, F44
nasal cavity, F46
nasal passages, F44
Nutrients, E43, F10,
F14–F15, F16–F17*,
F18, F30–F31, F40,
F60–F61
Nutrition information, F28
Nymph, A23*, A26–A27

O

Oasis, D25
Oceans, D9–D10, D16,
D18–D19, D36–D37,
D60, D64–D65*,
D67–D69
Offspring, A11, A18
Oil, C13, C18, C51
as pollutant, D59–D60
spill, D65*, D69
Oil well, D62
Omnivores, E18
Orbit, B46
Oxygen, A15, A43, F12

P

Palate, F44–F46
Pancreas, F60
Parasites, E54–E55
Parent, A10, A11, A42, A46
Parks, E67
Particles, C12, C13. *See also*
Matter: particles in.
Pasteur, Louis, F35
Pasteurization, F35
Peat, C59
People, E62–E63*, E66–E67.

See also Humans.
Perspiration, E72, F12. *See
also* Sweat.
Petal, A44–A45*, A46
Pill bug, E8–E9*, E12
Pistil, A44–A45*, A46, A47
Plains, E68
Planet, B46
Plant kingdom, A36
Plants, A6–A7*, A8–A9,
A36, A43, A44–A45*,
A54–A55, A58–A59*,
B28, C18, D70, E6–E7*,
E36, E40, E43, E56–E59
chemicals in, E56–E59
flowering, A38–A39*,
A44–A45*, A46
growth, D57*, D59
seed, A41, A46
swamp (source of coal),
C58–C59
Plaque, on teeth, F51, F53
Plastic
as pollutant, D60
Pollen, A44–A45*, A47–A48
Pollination, A47–A48
Pollutants, D58, D60, D69
Pollution
air, C50
laws against, D60,
D62–D63
water, D58–D61,
D62–D63, D64–D65*,
D69, D70, D78
Pond, E64
Prairie, E68
Precipitation, D16, D26
Predators, E27, E53–E55
Prey, E27
Producers, E16
role in living machine,
E20–E21
Protection, adaptation for,
E50–E54
in animals, E47*,
E48–E49,* E50, E52–E53
bitter taste, E51

Sunlight, A60, B28, B64–B66, C4, C16*, F52
  at equator, B64
  at North Pole and South Pole, B64
  spread of, B64–B65
Swallowing, F46–F47, F54–F55*, F58
Sweat, E72, E74. *See also* Perspiration.

T

Taproots, A42
Taste, F42–F43*
  taste buds, F42–F43*
Teeth, F13, F44, F48*, F49*, F50–F51, F53
  baby teeth, F48*
  tooth decay, F31, F51
Telescope, B11, B14–B17
Temperature, C14–C15*, C16*, C18, C20, C22, C24*, C26*, C35, C40*, C42, D12, E70–E71*, E72, E77, F36
Thermometer, C14–C15*, C16*, C24–C25*, C28, C40*
Thorns (of plants), A62
Throat, F46, F58
Tides, D64–D65*, D66*, D68–D69
Tongue, F42–F43*, F44–F46
Toothbrush, F49*, F51
Trait, A11
Trees, A41, A48, A50, A56–A57*
  branches, A53, A57
  trunk, A56–A57*
Tuber (of plant), A41, A43

U

Ultrasonic dental tool, F52
United States Department of Agriculture (USDA), F18, F21
Uranium, C53

V

Vacuum, C37
Vegetables, F20–F21, F30
Villi (of small intestine), F61
Vitamins, F10, F13, F14, F18, F28–F29
  Vitamin D, F14

W

Waste (food waste in body), F12, F61
Water, A42, A43, A48, A54, A60, B13, C18, C20, C24–C25*, C28, C30–C31*, C40*, C41*, C42–C44, D4, D6–D7*, D9–D10, D12*, D13*, D20–D21*, D24–D25, D26, D30, D32–D33*, D34–D35*, D36, D40–D41*, D48*, D49, D54, D70, D74, E64, E67, E72, E74–E75, F8–F9*, F10, F12, F18, F61
  chemicals in, D43, D45
  cost, D74
  distilled, D44
  droplets, C43
  evaporation, D15
  filtering, D46–D47*, D51
  fresh water, D9, D18, D20–D21*, D22–D23*, D51, D70
  as gas, D15, D17
  ground, D27
  hard water, D42*, D44
  in human body, D10
  as ice, D9
  as liquid, D15, D17
  in living things, D8*, D10
  minerals in, D43, D45
  salt, D9, D18–D19, D70
  saving, D61, D77–D78
  soft water, D42*, D44
  as solid, D15, D17
  surface water, D26, D48*
  use in homes, D11, D26, D37, D51, D72*, D73*, D74–D75
  use by towns and cities, D11, D26–D28, D37
  waste water (sewage), D52, D59
  wasting, D72*, D73*, D76
Water cycle, D13*, D17, D26, D52
Water mains, D38–D39
Water meter, D75
Water pipes, D30, D37, D39, D51, D75
Water pressure, D32–D33*, D36–D37, D51, D75
Water pumping station, D38
Water source, D20–D21*, D26–D28, D37, D38, D50
Water tower, D34–D35*, D51
Water treatment plant, D38, D50–D51, D75
Water vapor, C42–C43, D15, D17, D18–D19
Waves (of energy)
  light, C13
  sound, C13
Weather, B12, E76–E77
Weeds, D59
Well, D20–D21*, D24, D25, D28
Wetlands, E66–E67
Whales, A14, A32–A34
Wind, A42, A48, C11
Windpipe, F46–F47
Winter, E76–E78
Wood, C13, C18

X

X-rays, C19

CREDITS

Front Cover: *Design, Art Direction, and Production*: Design Five, NYC; *Photography:* Jade Albert; *Photography Production:* Picture It Corporation; *Illustration:* Burton Morris. **TOC:** Lori Anzalone; Terry Boles; Bob Brugger; Liz Conrad; A. J. Miller; Verlin Miller; Andrew Shiff; Peter Stallard; Jerry Zimmerman.

ILLUSTRATORS
UNIT 3A Chapter A1: Doreen Gay-Kassel: 24; Adam Mathews: 30, 31; Steve McInturff: 10, 11; A. J. Miller: 14, 15; Kathy Rusynyk: 8, 9. **Chapter A2:** Lori Anzalone: 46, 47, 63; Skip Baker: 53; Paul Blakey: 41, 42, 43, 56; Ka Botzis: 41; Julie Carpenter: 60; Eldon Doty: 40; Dan McGowan: 49, 52, 53, 54.

UNIT 3B Chapter B1: David Barber: 28; Jenny Campbell: 20, 22, 23; Richard Courtney: 7, 12, 13, 27, 29, 30, 31; Randy Hamblin: 10; A. J. Miller: 21; Robert Roper: 22; Stephen Wagner: 15. **Chapter B2:** Skip Baker: 42, 43; Tim Blough: 51, 52, 54; Michael Carroll: 38, 39, 52, 53, 54; Dennis Davidson: 46, 47; Eldon Doty: 48, 49; Verlin Miller: 39; Tom Powers: 37, 40, 45, 57; Susan Simon: 55, 56. **Chapter B3:** Liz Conrad: 64, 65, 66; Dennis Davidson: 77, 78; Eureka Cartography: 70; Traci Harmon: 70, 71; Uldis Klavins: 64, 65, 66; Jean and Mou–Sien Tseng: 68, 69, 76, 77, 78.

UNIT 3C Chapter C1: Larry Jost: 10, 11, 12, 13; Scott Luke: 8; Dave Winter: 21; Leslie Wolf: 20. **Chapter C2:** Terry Boles: 35; Randy Hamblin: 38, 39; Akio Matsuyoshi: 27, 28, 29, 45; Susan Melrath: 34; A. J. Miller: 35; Robert Roper: 37; Jim Turgeon: 42, 43, 44. **Chapter C3:** Ken Condon: 58, 62; Richard Courtney: 50, 51; Carlyn Iverson: 59; Nina Laden: 51, 52, 53; Joseph Scrofani: 54, 55, 60, 61, 63.

UNIT 3D Chapter D1: Bob Brugger: 9, 10, 11; Dan Clyne: 26, 27, 28; Glasgow & Assoc.: 11; Mike Meaker: 14, 15; Sergio Roffo: 24, 25; Robert Roper: 18, 19; Stephen Wagoner: 16, 17, 29. **Chapter D2:** Joe Boddy: 36; Larry Jost: 50, 51, 53; Robert Roper: 38, 39; Andrew Shiff: 43. **Chapter D3:** Terry Boles: 64, 65; Eldon Doty: 62, 63; Patrick Gnan: 68; Susan Johnston Carlson: 67, 70; Lazslo Kubini: 70; Bob Ostrum: 63; Tom Pansini: 58, 59, 76, 77, 78, 79; Robert Schuster: 61; Peter Stallard: 74, 75, 77, 78; Jerry Zimmerman: 67.

UNIT 3E Chapter E1: Higgins Bond: 11, 12; Jenny Campbell: 26, 27, 28, 29; Sarah Jane English: 30; Jackie Geyer: 27; Verlin Miller: 20, 21; Jim Owens: 16, 17, 18, 19; Jim Salvati: 32, 33, 35. **Chapter E2:** Jenny Campbell: 50, 51, 52, 53, 54, 55; Sarah Jane English: 56, 57, 59; Doreen Gay-Kassel: 49; Susan Melrath: 57; Phil Wilson: 44, 45. **Chapter E3:** Eldon Doty: 68, 69; Tina Fong: 72, 73; Jackie Geyer: 63, 66; Deborah Pinkney: 64, 65, 79; Robert Schuster: 76, 77.

UNIT 3F Chapter F1: Stephan Bauer: 23; Dan Brawner: 18, 19, 39; Eldon Doty: 34, 35; Sarah Jane English: 18, 19, 22; Joseph Scrofani: 10; Michael Sloan: 30, 31; Stephen Wagner: 17; Gary Yealdall: 14, 15. **Chapter F2:** Dan Clyne: 52, 53; Robert Margulies: 45, 46, 47, 58, 59, 60, 62, 63; Leonard Morgan: 50, 51; Julie Noonan: 56, 57; Andrew Shiff: 45, 46, 47, 59, 60, 62.

Glossary: Richard Courtney, A. J. Miller, Robert Margulies, Andy Meyer, Robert Roper, Stephen Wagner

Handbook: Laurie Hamilton, Catherine Leary.

PHOTOGRAPHS
All photographs by Silver Burdett Ginn (SBG) unless otherwise noted.

Unit A Opener 1–3: *border* G. I. Bernard/Animals Animals. 2: Grant Huntington for SBG; *l.* © M. Reardon/Photo Researchers, Inc. **Chapter 1** 4: *bkgd.* Fred Hirschmann; *inset* Erik Hill/Anchorage Daily News. 8: Dwight R. Kuhn. 14: E. R. Degginger/Color-Pics, Inc. 16: *t.* E. R. Degginger/Color-Pics, Inc.; *b.* Frans Lanting/Minden Pictures. 17: *l.* Chick Maste;*r r.* Gil Taylor/Chick Master 18: *t.* Hans & Judy Beste/Animals Animals; *b.r.* © M. Reardon/Photo Researchers, Inc. 19: *t.* Miriam Austerman/Animals Animals; *m.* Michio Hoshino/Minden Pictures; *b.* Frans Lanting/Minden Pictures. 23: *b.l.* J. H. Robinson/Animals Animals; *b.r.* R. Mendez/Animals Animals. 24: Courtesy Evelyn O'Shea. 25: *t.l.* E. R. Degginger/Animals Animals; *t.r.* Patti Murray/Animal Animals; *b.l., b.r.* Patti Murray/Animals Animals. 27: *t.l.* Raymond A. Mendez/Animals Animals; *t.r.* John Pontier/Animals Animals; *b.* © David & Hayes Norris/Photo Researchers, Inc. 30: Anne Heimann. 31: *t.* Dwight R. Kuhn; *b.l.* Anne Heimann; *b.r.* Trevor Barrett/Animals Animals. 32: Flip Nicklin/Minden Pictures. 33: Jeff Foott/DRK Photo. 34: Michio Hoshino/Minden Pictures. **Chapter 2** 36: *bkgd.* Antonio M. Rosario/The Image Bank; *inset* Jill Krementz. 38–39: Grant Huntington for SBG. 42: *t.* S. Nielsen/Imagery; *m.* Runk/Schoenberger/Grant Heilman Photography; *b.* E. R. Degginger/Color-Pics, Inc. 43: Dwight R. Kuhn. 44–45: Grant Huntington for SBG. 48: *l.* Jim Strauser/Grant Heilman Photography; *r.* Jim Strawser/Grant Heilman Photography. 50: Grant Huntington for SBG; 51: *t.l.* Grant

Huntington for SBG; *t.r.* E. R. Degginger/Color-Pics, Inc.; *m.r.* E. R. Degginger/Color-Pics, Inc.; *b.l.* Grant Huntington for SBG; *b.r.* E. R. Degginger/Color-Pics, Inc. 55: *t.l.* David Austen/Tony Stone Images; *t.r.* Mark Stouffer/Earth Scenes; *b.* Don Pitcher/Stock Boston. 57–59: Grant Huntington for SBG. 60: Barry L. Runk/Grant Heilman Photography. 61: *l.* Runk/Schoenberger/Grant Heilman Photography. 62: *l.* Runk/Schoenberger/Grant Heilman Photography; *r.* Jim Strauser/Grant Heilman Photography.

Unit B Opener 1–3: *border* Frank P. Rossotto. 2: *t.* George Post. **Chapter 1** 4–5: *bkgd.* Lick Observatory; *inset* Victor Aleman/2 Mun-Dos Communications. 6: Grant Huntington for SBG. 11: *t.* NASA; *b.* H. R. Bramaz/Peter Arnold. 12: NASA/The Stock Market. 13: NASA. 14: Roger Ressmeyer/Starlight. 16: Photri. 17: NASA. 18–19: Grant Huntington for SBG. 23: *l.* NASA/Starlight (Photo by Neil Armstrong); *r.* © NASA/Science Source/Photo Researchers, Inc. 24–26: Grant Huntington for SBG. 29: *t.* Photri; *b.* © Pekka Parviainen/Science Photo Library/Photo Researchers, Inc. 30: *t.* National Solar Observatory/Sacramento Peak; *b.* NASA/F. Rossotto/StockTrek. **Chapter 2** 32–33: *bkgd.* E. R. Degginger/Color-Pics, Inc. 34: Grant Huntington for SBG. 35: *t.* Grant Huntington for SBG; *b.* E. R. Degginger/Color-Pics, Inc. 37: *l.* Grant Huntington for SBG; *m.* Grant Huntington for SBG; *r.* Grant Huntington for SBG. 38: © Sylvain Grandadam/Photo Researchers, Inc. 40: Dennis Cox/ChinaStock. 40–41: *bkgd.* Robert Holmes; *inset* Oddo & Sinibaldi/The Stock Market. 41: *t.l.* Robert Holmes; *t.m.* D & J McClurg/Bruce Coleman; *t.r.* Norman Owen Tomalin/Bruce Coleman; *b.* © Dale E. Boyer/Photo Researchers, Inc. 46: Thomas Hooper/© National Geographic Society. 50: Grant Huntington for SBG. 52: NASA. **Chapter 3** 58–59: *bkgd.* John Gerlach/Tom Stack & Associates; *inset* Doranne Jacobson. 60: Ken Karp for SBG. 61: Ken Karp for SBG. 62: Ken Karp for SBG. 63: Ken Karp for SBG. 67: *bkgd.* Tibor Bognar/The Stock Market; *inset* Robert Frerck/Odyssey Productions; *inset* D. Donne Bryant. 68: Superstock. 69: Courtesy, National Maritime Museum. 71: *t.* Superstock; *b.* Brian Stablyk/Tony Stone Images. 73: *t.* George Post; *b.* S. Nielsen/Imagery. 74: Ken Karp for SBG. 75: Ken Karp for SBG. 76: Ken Sakamonto/Black Star. 79: Ken Karp for SBG.

Unit C Opener 1–3: *border* David Barnes/The Stock Market. 2: Grant Huntington for SBG. **Chapter 1** 4–5: *bkgd.* Camerique/H. Armstrong Roberts; *inset* Ruth Tenzer Feldman. 6–10: Grant Huntington for SBG. 11: Alan Oddie/PhotoEdit. 12–16: Grant Huntington for SBG; 17: David Phillips for SBG. 18: *t.l.* Joe Cornish/Tony Stone Images; *t.r* Superstock; *b.l.* David Phillips for SBG; *b.r.* Phil Degginger/Color-Pics, Inc. 19: *l.* The Image Bank; *r.* Bob Krist/Tony Stone Images. **Chapter 2** 23–24: *bkgd.* Renato Rotolo/Liaison International; *inset* ©Bob Halinen/Anchorage Daily News/Liaison International. 36: *l.* Richard Hutchings for SBG; *r.* Isaac Geib/Grant Heilman Photography. 38: *t.* Barry L. Runk/Grant Heilman Photography. 38–39: *bkgd.* John Shaw/Tom Stack & Associates. 39: *b.* Climb High/Signs and Symbols. 42: *t.* Richard Hutchings for SBG. 43: *t.* Arthur D'Arazien/The Image Bank. 44: *t.* David R. Frazier ; *b.m., b.r.* Grant Huntington for SBG. **Chapter 3** 46–47: *bkgd.* Comstock. 52: *t.* Comstock; *b.* Thomas Braise/The Stock Market. 53: *t.* John Edwards/Tony Stone Images; *b.* Zefa-Streichan/The Stock Market. 54: Wolfgang Kaehler. 59: *t.* E. R. Degginger/Color-Pics, Inc.; *m.t.* E. R. Degginger/Color-Pics, Inc.; *m.b.* E. R. Degginger/Bruce Coleman; *b.* E. R. Degginger/Bruce Coleman.

Unit D Opener 1–3: *border* Robert Reiff/FPG International. 2: **Chapter 1** 4–5: *bkgd.* © Jim Zipp/Photo Researchers, Inc.; *l.* Kyle McLellan/© National Geographic Society; *r.* © Jeff Lepore/Photo Researchers, Inc. 10: NASA/Tom Stack & Associates. 11: *t.l.* Jeff Smith/The Image Bank; *t.r.* © 1996 Jim Richardson/Woodfin Camp & Associates; *b.l.* Comstock; *b.r.* Merritt Vincent/PhotoEdit. 24: *l.* Steve McCutcheon/Alaska Pictorial; *r.* Wolfgang Kaehler. 25: *t.* ©1996 Sylvia Johnson/Woodfin Camp & Associates; *m.* Wolfgang Kaehler; *b.* E. R. Degginger/Color-Pics, Inc. 26: Mark Segal/Tony Stone Images. 27: Sobel/Klonsky/The Image Bank. 28: Bob Daemmrich Photography. **Chapter 2** 30–34: *bkgd.* John David Fleck/Liaison International; *inset* © David M. Grossman/Photo Researchers, Inc. 32: Ken Karp for SBG. 35: *b.* Mitchell Funk/The Image Bank; *(t.)* Ken Karp for SBG; 36: The Image Bank. 40–42: Ken Karp for SBG. 44: Hans Reinhard/Bruce Coleman. 45: Keith Wood/Tony Stone Images. 46–48: Ken Karp for SBG. 49: *l.* Jerry Lessen/Bruce Coleman; *m.t.l.* E. R. Degginger/Color-Pics, Inc.; *m.b.l.* Brian Parker/Tom Stack & Associates; *m.r.* © London School of Hygiene and Tropical Medicine/Science Photo Library/Photo Researchers, Inc.; *t.r.* Moredon Animal Health Ltd./Science Photo Library/Photo Researchers, Inc.; *b.r.* © Moredon Animal Health Ltd./Science Photo Library/Photo Researchers, Inc. 52: David Madison/Bruce Coleman. **Chapter 3** 54–55: © Antonin Kratochvil/*Discover* Magazine. 56–57: Grant Huntington for SBG. 61: Kay Chernush/The Image Bank. 65–66: Grant Huntington for SBG. 69: *l.* © Andrew J. Martinez/Photo Researchers, Inc.; *r.* © J. Martinez/Photo Researchers, Inc. 71: Timothy A. Murphy/The Image Bank. 73: Grant Huntington for SBG. 74: Richard Hutchings for SBG.

Unit E Opener 1–3: *border* John Gerlach/Tom Stack & Associates. 2: *l.* Marty Snyderman. **Chapter 1** 4–5: *bkgd.* Tom Bean/Tony Stone Images; *inset* © Melinda M. Hutton. 6–7: Grant Huntington for SBG. 8: *l.* Donald Specker/Animals Animals; *r.* Grant Huntington for SBG. 9: Grant Huntington for SBG. 10: Doug Perrine/DRK Photo. 12: *t.* Michael Fogden/DRK Photo; *b.* Al Grotell. 13: *t.* Stephen J. Krasemann/Peter Arnold; *b.* © Dr. Jeremy Burgess/Science Photo Library/Photo Researchers, Inc. 14–15: Grant Huntington for SBG. 16: *l.* D. Cavagnaro-DRK Photo; *m.* © Farrell Grehan/Photo Researchers, Inc.; *r.* N. H. Cheatham/DRK Photo. 17: *t.* Hans Pfletschinger-/Peter Arnold; *b.* Jim Brandenburg/Minden Pictures. 18: *t.* © Tim Davis/Photo Researchers, Inc.; *b.* © Tom Bledsoe/Photo Researchers, Inc. 19: *t.* Breck P. Kent/Animals Animals; *b.* Scott Nielsen/Imagery. 22–25: Grant Huntington for SBG. 26: *l.* © James Steinberg/Photo Researchers, Inc.; *m.* © Gary Retherford/Photo Researchers, Inc.; *r.* Zig Leszczynski/Animals Animals. 27: *l.* Ted Levin/Animals Animals; *r.* Joe McDonald/Animals Animals. 28: *t.l.* Stephen J. Krasemann/DRK Photo; *t.r.* M. P. Kahl/DRK Photo; *b.l.* Stephen Dalton/Animals Animals; *b.r.* John

**This
Read, Listen, & Wonder
book belongs to:**

_____

_____

_____

CANDLEWICK PRESS

Greater horseshoe bat

(Rhinolophus ferrumequinum)

Greater bulldog bat

(Noctilio leporinus)

White fruit bats

(Ectophylla alba)

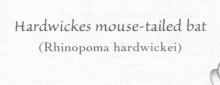

Common vampire bat

(Desmodus rotundus)

Spotted bat

(Euderma maculatum)

Hardwickes mouse-tailed bat

(Rhinopoma hardwickei)

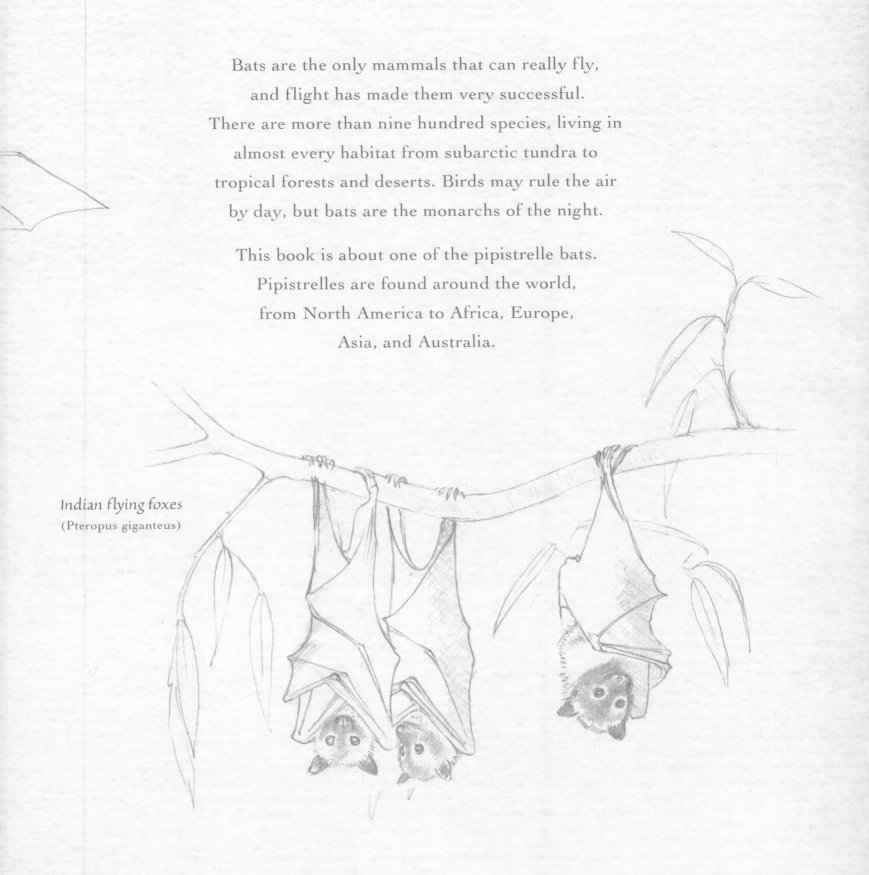

Bats are the only mammals that can really fly,
and flight has made them very successful.
There are more than nine hundred species, living in
almost every habitat from subarctic tundra to
tropical forests and deserts. Birds may rule the air
by day, but bats are the monarchs of the night.

This book is about one of the pipistrelle bats.
Pipistrelles are found around the world,
from North America to Africa, Europe,
Asia, and Australia.

Indian flying foxes
(Pteropus giganteus)

For Henry Venner Woodcock and his big brothers,
Alfie and Thomas
N. D.

For Ailsa
S. F-D.

Text copyright © 2001 by Nicola Davies
Illustrations copyright © 2001 by Sarah Fox-Davies

First U.S. paperback edition with CD 2008

The Library of Congress has cataloged the hardcover edition as follows:

Davies, Nicola.
Bat loves the night / Nicola Davies ; illustrated by Sarah Fox-Davies. — 1st U.S. ed.
p. cm.
Summary: Bat wakes up, flies into the night, uses the echoes of her
voice to navigate, hunts for her supper, and returns to her roost to feed her baby.
ISBN 978-0-7636-1202-3 (hardcover)
1. Bats — Juvenile fiction. [1. Bats — Fiction.] I. Fox-Davies, Sarah, ill. II. Title.
PZ10.3.D2865 Bat 2001
[E] — dc21   00-066681

ISBN 978-0-7636-2438-5 (paperback)
ISBN 978-0-7636-3863-4 (paperback with CD)

2 4 6 8 10 9 7 5 3

Printed in China

This book was typeset in Cochin and Sanvito.
The illustrations were done in watercolor and pencil.

Candlewick Press
2067 Massachusetts Avenue
Cambridge, Massachusetts 02140

visit us at www.candlewick.com

BAT
LOVES
THE
NIGHT

Nicola Davies

illustrated by Sarah Fox-Davies

CANDLEWICK PRESS
CAMBRIDGE, MASSACHUSETTS

Bat is waking,
upside down as usual,
hanging by her toenails.

Her beady eyes open.
Her pixie ears twitch.

She shakes her
thistledown fur.

She unfurls her wings,
made of skin so fine the finger bones
inside show through.

The pipistrelle bat's
body is no bigger than
your thumb.

A bat's wing is its
arm and hand.
Four extra-long fingers
support the skin of the wing.

Bats' toes are shaped like hooks,
so it's no effort for a bat to hang
upside down.

Now she unhooks her toes
and drops into black space.
With a sound like a tiny umbrella
opening, she flaps her wings.

Bat is flying.

Out!

Out under the broken tile
into the nighttime garden.

Over bushes, under trees,
between fence posts,
through the tangled hedge
she swoops untouched.
Bat is at home in the darkness
as a fish is in the water.
She doesn't need to see —
she can hear where she is going.

*Bats can see. But in the dark, good ears are
more useful than eyes.*

12

Bat shouts as she flies, louder
than a hammer blow, higher than a
squeak. She beams her voice around her
like a flashlight, and the echoes come
singing back. They carry a sound picture
of all her voice has touched.
Listening hard, Bat can hear every
detail, the smallest twigs, the
shape of leaves.

Using sound to find your way
like this is called echolocation.
The noise bats make when they
shout is too high for humans to hear.

14

Gliding and fluttering
back and forth,
she shouts her torch of
sound among the trees,
listening for her supper.

All is still. . . .

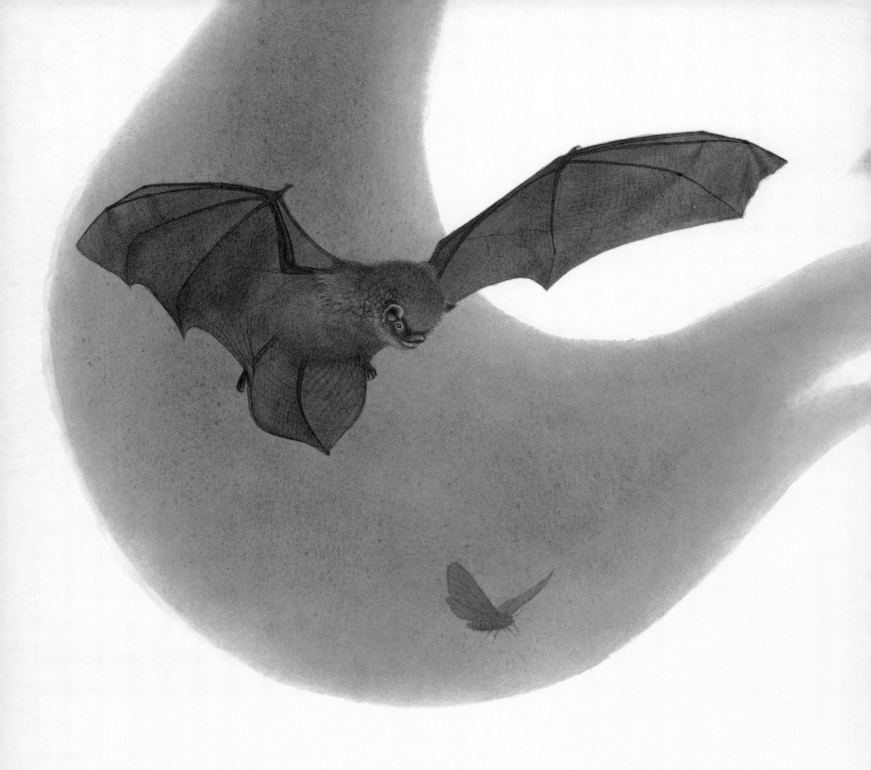

Then a fat moth takes flight below her.

Bat plunges, fast as blinking, and grabs it in her open mouth.

But the moth's pearly scales are moon-dust slippery. It slithers from between her teeth.

Bat dives, nets it with a wing tip, scoops it to her mouth.

This time she bites hard.
Its wings fall away, like the
wrapper from a candy.
In a moment the moth is eaten.
Bat sneezes.
The dusty scales got up her nose.

A bat can eat dozens of big moths
in a single night — or thousands of tiny
flies, gnats, and mosquitoes.

Most species of bats eat
insects, but there are some
that eat fruit, fish, frogs,
even blood!

Hunting time has run out.
The dark will soon be gone.
In the east, the sky is getting light.
It's past Bat's bedtime.

The place where bats sleep in the day is called a roost.
It can be in a building, a cave, or a tree, so long as it's dry and safe.

She flies to the roof in the last shadows
and swoops in under the broken tile.

Inside, there are squeakings.
Fifty hungry batlings hang in a huddle,
hooked to a rafter by oversized feet.
Bat lands and pushes in among them,
toes first, upside down again.

Baby bats can't fly.
Sometimes mother bats carry their babies when
they go out, but mostly the babies stay behind in the roost
and crowd together to keep warm.

Bat knows her baby's voice, and calls to it.

The velvet scrap batling climbs aboard and clings to Bat's fur by its coat-hanger feet.

Wrapped in her
leather wings, the
baby suckles
Bat's milk.

Baby bats drink mother's milk until
they learn to fly at a few weeks old.
Then they can leave the roost
at night to find their own food.

Outside, the birds are singing.
The flowers turn their faces to the sun.
But inside the roof hole,
the darkness stays.
Bat dozes with her batling,
waiting.

Bats are nocturnal. That means they rest by day
and come out at night to search for food.

When the tide of night rises again,
Bat will wake and plunge
into the blackness, shouting.

Bat loves the night.

Index

Look up the pages to find
out about all these batty things.
Don't forget to look at both
kinds of words —
this kind and
this kind.

Mexican freetail bat

(Tadarida brasiliensis)